The Golden Puck

Lane Walker

LOCAL LEGENDS
www.bakkenbooks.com

The Golden Puck by Lane Walker
First Edition
Copyright © 2024 Lane Walker

Cover Design: Roger Betka

All rights reserved. This book is protected under the copyright laws of the United States of America. This book may not be copied or reprinted for commercial gain or profit.

ISBN 978-1-963915-08-2
For Worldwide Distribution
Printed in the U.S.A.

Published by Bakken Books
2024
www.bakkenbooks.com

*This book is dedicated to
Caleb and Caiden.*

In a world where the roar of the crowd and the clash of sticks define the game, your resilience and courage shine. In the pages of this book, may you find echoes of your own courage and perseverance, and may it serve as a tribute to the impact you've had on everyone around you.

www.bakkenbooks.com

Math adventures for kids

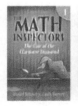  

History adventures for kids

Space adventures for kids

Humorous adventures for kids

-1-
Prologue

My breath floated lazily in the cold, damp air.

I couldn't see it, but I could *feel* the cold.

Hockey arenas across the world are typically cold, but the Calumet Colosseum is exceptionally frigid.

My body started to fidget and tremble.

"Caleb, breathe! You got this," I said to myself. Talking to myself was common for me, especially when I was playing hockey.

Deep down, I knew I couldn't convince myself of a lie. I wasn't shaking because of the frigid temperatures inside the colosseum.

Am I going to lose the game for my team? Can I even help them at all?

I was a shell of the hockey player I once had been.

I started playing hockey when I was five years old. I remember falling a lot at first, but my dad kept encouraging me. He would look me square in my eyes and say, "Son, it will be hard at first, but worth it. You will fall down. Don't stay down; you have to get back up every time."

I thought back to those early memories on the ice.

Dad's words were just as true now as they had been eight years ago. Sports are designed to teach life lessons. During those early moments on the ice as a five-year-old, Dad was teaching me to never give up, no matter how much it hurt or how many times I fell.

The past eight years of hockey have reinforced Dad's never-give-up attitude. After that first day, I fell in love with hockey. I skated every chance I got, sometimes even twice a day.

Dad was right, the next day had been easier. Even though I still fell and ran into the wall, skating was slightly better than the day before. After going to the rink five days in a row, I fell in love with hockey.

Not just skating or playing the game, I loved every aspect of being on the ice.

When I was on the ice, time seemed to stand still. My mind was at peace, and I was in the one place where I was truly happy. I felt a certain freedom as I pushed my skates into the ice. I had played other sports, but none of them gave me the same feeling I had when I was skating. Every time I laced up my skates or slipped on my number 26 jersey, I was in my zone.

I have played in over a hundred hockey games. My teams have won huge games, championships, and even a national tournament in Pittsburgh, Pennsylvania. In fact, mine was the only team from Michigan to win in Pittsburgh. That game was one of the best memories I have ever had.

But those exciting games and memories are now in the past. The natural feeling of gliding across the ice seems so much harder now.

I thought all those years of practice and ice time would pay off as I got older. I played travel hockey nine months out of the year. Even with all the experience and hard work, none of that could prepare me for the roadblocks I had been forced to face this year. I thought fourteen would be one of the coolest years of my life.

This was the first time I had ever felt cold on the ice. In the past, I was always hot from all the gear and constant movement, but not today...

My toes were numb, and I was so cold I could feel the iciness in my bones. As I waited, I wrestled with self-doubt. I was shocked that I had been invited to go into the game at all, but I was.

After everything I've gone through the past couple months, is playing in this game going to be another heartbreak? How will I perform on ice right now? The pressure from the situation was only adding to the overwhelming feeling I had in the pit of my stomach.

I stumbled as I left the players' box and skated toward the center of the ice. My legs shook, and my feet felt like concrete blocks. *There's no getting out of this.*

I was cold, but not because of the temperature in the ice arena. The game was in the third and final period; only twenty seconds remained in the game, and the score was tied.

It was the first time I had played in the game, and the game was on the line. *These past four weeks have been the most difficult in my life both mentally and physically. How could Coach even think of putting me in with the championship game tied?*

Will I be the one to lose it all for my team?

I don't want to be the reason our team loses.

-2-

Hockey is a huge part of my life. Not only do I enjoy playing the game, but I also love watching it. My favorite team is the Detroit Red Wings. Growing up in Michigan, the Red Wings are most people's team of choice. My love for the Red Wings started before I fell in love with the game of hockey.

My parents showed me pictures taken at the hospital on the day that I was born. This small baby with eyes wide open staring at the camera is lying in a crib with a custom newborn Red Wings jersey and a miniature hockey stick nestled neatly beside him.

My mom had learned to fall in love with hockey as well. She had met my dad in college and fallen

The Golden Puck

in love with this long-haired forward on the club hockey team. My dad was a good, high-level player but not quite good enough to make hockey his full-time job.

Dad was All-State in high school. After graduating, he attended Saginaw Valley State University (SVSU) in Saginaw, Michigan, a smaller Division Two college. Their only hockey team was a club sport, meaning they didn't offer scholarships or travel on fancy charter buses. Instead, the SVSU team played other club teams around the state.

Dad's team was made up of a lot of guys who loved to be on the ice. Mom loved telling me stories of her nights spent watching Dad play and joking about how often she had to watch him sit in the penalty box...

With these roots, it was only natural that as I got older, my love for hockey grew. It seemed like life was perfect for our family. My dad owned a construction company and was one of the best builders in our area. Mom was a teacher and loved washing her son's stinky hockey gear.

My dad had coached every hockey team I played on. He was a great coach and possessed a fantastic knowledge of the game.

By the time I was twelve, I had stopped playing other sports. Like most kids in my class, I had tried baseball, basketball, and football. I was pretty good at football because I was fast and coordinated from all the years I had spent skating.

I liked the physical contact of football, but even though aspects were similar to hockey, I had no interest in playing anything but hockey. The way I see it, hockey is the perfect blend of physicality, passing, hand-eye coordination, and teamwork. It combines so many aspects of other sports, but we also have checking! Knowing I was born to be on the ice, I stopped playing other sports one by one until finally, in the eighth grade, I focused all my time on playing hockey.

Whenever I stepped on the ice, I couldn't help but smile. It was the one place on earth where everything felt right, and it was where I was at my best.

- 3 -

I was really looking forward to my eighth-grade year.

When I was three, Dad told us we were moving from Saginaw to a small town named Bad Axe on the tip of the thumb of Michigan. I remember being excited about the town's name. *How many kids can say their hometown is called Bad Axe?*

Usually at hockey tournaments, someone would always ask where our team was from. Every time we said, "Bad Axe," we got incredulous looks. I always knew the next question would be "Bad Axe? Why is your town called *that*?"

It wasn't until I was older that I learned about the founders of Bad Axe and other interesting facts about my small town. Our fourth-grade history teacher, Mr. Heart, loved to teach about Michigan history. In fact, he spent an entire week teaching us about the history of Bad Axe.

In 1861 two surveyors were in Huron County, mapping out possible locations for a new road to connect the area to the rest of the state. While surveying, the two came to a tree where they found a heavily used and badly damaged ax. One of the men wrote "Bad Axe Camp" on their map and quickly made a sign, placing it by the trail. From that point on, the area was known as Bad Axe.

Bad Axe was originally settled in the 1830s as a lumbering community. Michigan is known for its towering white pines and its logging industry, which attract people to the area.

I love my hometown. Our area has a population of around 3,000 and is primarily an agricultural area. Farmers plant soybeans, corn, sugar beets, and various other crops. One of the greatest aspects of my town is being only ten miles from Lake Huron, the second largest of the Great Lakes. The crystal-clear waters, gorgeous shorelines, and sandy beaches are a great draw during the hot summer months.

The climate and beach make Huron County the perfect spot for summer travelers. The population of the county triples from the tons of tourists visiting our area during the summer months. I like my Michigan summers and enjoy spending time at the beach, but I love the winter…

Michigan winters can be brutal, and living near Lake Huron means that our winter months are full of snow, ice, and cold. Toward the end of October, temperatures drop, and the talk of snow whispers from all the lips of school kids hoping for a snow day. The wind blows strong out of the west, and it takes on the role of villain, wreaking havoc on anyone brave enough to venture outside.

I didn't worry about any of those aspects. The colder temperatures and weather shift announced the arrival of my favorite season—hockey season.

It was time for Barn Burner hockey! This was the year we were going to win the Golden Puck!

a# -4-

The Golden Puck Tournament is held yearly during the first weekend of December in Calumet, Michigan. The tournament is only open to eighth-grade teams. Since it is the last travel tournament before the players move to high school, the Golden Puck is like the Super Bowl of eighth-grade hockey, and only the best are allowed in.

No team from Huron County had ever won the national tournament in Calumet. Teams from all over the United States and Canada traveled every year to the tiny town of Calumet for a chance to be crowned the Golden Puck champion!

The hockey is high-level, but what really makes the Golden Puck Tournament so special is the colosseum where the game is played. The Calumet Colosseum was built in 1913 and is one of the oldest and most historic hockey arenas in the world. The facility opened as an indoor roller rink before being converted to an ice rink.

The colosseum has hosted and witnessed memorable moments in hockey history. Several professional hockey teams from the National Hockey League held exhibition games there to celebrate its rich history. My favorite team, the Detroit Red Wings, has played there. I remember a couple years ago watching the Red Wings play a preseason game at the colosseum. The Wings won an NHL award, and the city of Calumet received $150,000 for repairs and renovations.

The Golden Puck Tournament was first held in March 1921. The tournament was established in honor of a nationally known football player named George Gipp, also known as "the Gipper." George grew up near Calumet and played football at the University of Notre Dame from 1917-1920. The Gipper was recognized for his exceptional skills on the football field. In December of 1920, the twenty-five-year-old suddenly passed away due to an infection.

Legendary Notre Dame Coach Knute Rockne adapted a request made by George from his deathbed in a speech to rally his "Fighting Irish" team to victory.

> "Rock, some time, Rock, when the team is up against it—and the breaks are beating the boys—tell them to go out there with all they got and win just one for the Gipper... I don't know where I'll be then, Rock, but I'll know about it—and I'll be happy."[1]

The second half of the game, the score was tied 6-6, and Rockne shared Gipper's story and his request with his team. Inspired by Rockne's story of Gipp's request, the team rallied and won the game 12-6. From that day on, the speech "Win One for the Gipper," became an iconic part of Notre Dame history. The story of George Gipp was immortalized in a 1940 movie, *Knute Rockne, All American*.

The Golden Puck

The world loved the Gipper, and none more than the people of Calumet in the Upper Peninsula.

After Gipper's untimely death, the town council of Calumet established the Golden Puck Tournament in honor of George Gipp's life. The tournament's name originated from Gipp's helmet at Notre Dame made of pure 14-karat gold! Instead of the black hockey pucks commonly used in games, the tournament founders instituted using a 24-karat golden puck for the championship game.

Every year when the puck drops for the championship game, it remains the only tournament that uses a golden puck. The winning team is given the puck as the trophy. The puck is said to be worth almost $5,000, but to the winning coaches and players, it's priceless.

Teams from around the world line up for a chance to compete to be the champions of the Golden Puck Tournament. Only the best of the best take the rare trophy home.

Knowing that the golden puck had never been claimed for Bad Axe or Huron County, our team had talked of winning the puck for the past four years. We frequently discussed what we would do when it was finally our turn to play in the tournament. Our team was consumed with winning the Golden Puck.

---

[1]"Knute Rockne's 'Win One for the Gipper' Speech,' " December 8, 2023, *University of Notre Dame Archives*, https://archives.nd.edu/research/texts/rocknespeech.htm, accessed May 9, 2024.

- 5 -

My hockey team was named the Barn Burners and consisted of kids from my hometown and other locals in our county. Though most of the players grew up and lived in Huron County, a couple of kids traveled from neighboring counties to play on our team because we were so good.

Our team had fifteen players, and five of them came from Bad Axe. My closest and best friends, Dalton, Lucas, Nathan, and Colin, were my teammates. Those who attended our school had nicknamed our group "The Frozen Five" because we were always huddled together, talking about hockey.

The month of November was circled on all of our calendars. For me, it couldn't come fast enough. All fall, the Frozen Five planned and prepared for the upcoming hockey season. Some of the guys played fall sports like football, but the love we all shared was exclusively for the winter hockey season.

We were chomping at the bit to get on the ice. Hockey practice always started in mid-November, with our first tournament taking place at the end of the month.

Not only did November signify the first practice of the travel hockey season, but it was also the start of deer hunting season. Both were big deals in the life of rural Michigan middle schoolers.

November 15 in Michigan is practically a state holiday. While it might not be an official holiday, the opening of the firearm deer season is full of tradition for both hunters and non-hunters alike. Buck poles and chili dinners are as common as Easter eggs and candy canes. Our family loved to hunt deer, and I looked forward to heading out to the woods with my dad and brother.

Yes, November 15 was always an exciting day,

but the one I really got geeked up for was November 16, the first day of hockey practice for the Barn Burners. The anticipation for the start of hockey season was pouring out of the Frozen Five. The entire school was filled with excitement for the upcoming Barn Burners hockey season.

For those who didn't know or care about hockey, that all changed when Dalton cleared his throat to present his speech in our eighth-grade English class. Dalton, who was large and agile, served as our goalie.

Our English assignment had been to prepare and present a five-minute speech in front of the whole class. Dalton's speech was all about the Golden Puck Tournament and the history of the Calumet Colosseum's ice rink. His delivery was motivating and energetic, portraying exactly how we all felt about this year's tournament. Near the end of his speech, he cleared his throat. He clearly had something to add that he felt was important—something so awesome that he wanted the entire class to sit up and take notice.

He eased forward, giving the teacher a side-eyed glance before ending his speech. "This is the year. Led by the Frozen Five, our team is going to deliver the Golden Puck to Huron County for the first time ever! We are coming home with that puck in December," he said proudly.

An eerie silence settled over the room as the whole class sat staring open-mouthed at Dalton. Finally, a couple of kids at the back of the room snickered, and a low murmur spread over the class.

Someone yelled, "You know no one from Bad Axe has ever won that tournament."

Mr. Smith, our English teacher, finally stopped the increasing rowdiness with a quick, modest, clap of his hands.

"Okay, class! Thank you, Dalton. Does anyone have questions about Dalton's report?" he asked.

I scanned the room, hoping that no one would say anything else. Dalton had merely said what the Frozen Five had been talking about for the past couple years. We wanted to be the first team to bring home the Golden Puck, but I had no idea he would say it out loud and so confidently. Our dream was to win, but it was *our* dream. I didn't think the rest of our English class had to know about it.

Suddenly a hand shot up in the middle of the classroom.

"Yes, Rose, go ahead," said Mr. Smith.

"Some pretty good teams from here have played in that tournament. In fact, my older brother Scotty was on a way better team than you guys. Do you really think your team can win the tournament?"

Dalton, now embarrassed by Rose's tone and comment, backpedaled. His face turned a strawberry red as he scanned the room, trying to think of what his next words were going to be. Instead, he froze and didn't know what to do or how to answer. Watching one of my best friends standing alone and embarrassed was painful.

That was the thing with the Frozen Five; we were never alone, and we always had each other's backs. So I responded with the first thing that popped into my mind.

I stood up and shouted, "Yeah, we are going to win! I guarantee it." I couldn't believe the words came out of my mouth until I heard myself saying them.

What did I just do?

A look of relief washed over Dalton's face as I attempted to save him from even more embarrassment.

An awkward silence lasted only a couple minutes before we both were saved by the bell, releasing us from class. Little did I know that Dalton's speech was only the beginning of one of the hardest months of my life.

-6-

I got up and exited the English classroom as fast as I could. I tried to sneak through the main hallway, but as I rounded the corner toward my history class, I felt a solid tug on my left arm.

"Why did you say that?" Lucas asked in a serious tone.

I turned, and our entire group—all the members of the Frozen Five—were facing me, and they didn't look happy.

"I was trying to help Dalton; I didn't want him to feel bad," I said.

"Thanks for that support, by the way. I had no idea what I was going to say," Dalton quickly replied.

"Do you know how much pressure you put on all of us—on our team? You guaranteed a victory in one of the biggest, toughest hockey tournaments in the world!" Lucas exclaimed.

Lucas was one to get emotional quickly, and that tendency was showing now.

He added, "All my dad has talked about is how we are the ones who could finally bring the Golden Puck home. I am already getting nervous about it."

"Chill, Lucas, it's all good. Caleb is right. I feel the same way; we are going to win," said Nathan.

Shocked, the four of us turned toward the one member of the Frozen Five who was typically quiet and unassuming. He was the last person on earth who would say something like that. In fact, knowing his personality caused all of us to listen even more carefully when he talked. He was a boy of few words, but when he spoke, his words always carried a lot of wisdom.

Anxious to hear what Nathan was thinking, Lucas invited, "Go on."

"We have a good team, and Caleb is one of the

best centers in the entire state. If he thinks we will win, I do too," said Nathan.

There was a short pause.

"Okay, then I guess we plan on winning. We have talked about it for a while, but now the whole school knows," said Lucas.

"Who cares?" piped up Colin from the opposite side of the group.

"I care for one; it matters to me if Rose runs her mouth about us at school. Because she tends to be overly talkative, she reveals too much information, and you guys all know that," said Lucas.

Pressure has a funny influence when it comes to life and sports. My dad always told me that pressure can be used to crush a car or make diamonds. At the time, I was only saying how I felt—how we all felt. The Frozen Five was devoted to bringing home the trophy to Huron County.

After Dalton's speech today and my strong statement, I was fairly sure that we would be hearing a lot more about the end-of-the-year hockey tournament. The tournament was still over a month away.

Lane Walker

What the Frozen Five didn't know was, there would be added pressure to win the Golden Puck Tournament.

- 7 -

After school, the Frozen Five loaded a school bus to be dropped off at our local ice rink for practice and tryouts. The first two days of practice were always held as tryouts in case new people wanted to try out to join our team.

We only kept the best fifteen players; anyone not making the team would have to play on a local club team. We knew who most of the guys on the team would be since we had thirteen Barn Burners coming back from last year's team. I figured the other players would fight it out to see who would make our team. Usually around twenty-five to thirty kids tried out for our travel team. Tryouts were always high energy and action-packed.

Typically, the same local kids from our area showed up, though once in a while someone new would attend. We rarely found a top line player at the tryouts.

As we walked into the locker room, I headed to where I saw my hockey bag lying against the lockers. *Dad always leaves it in the same place.* We hurried to get ready, excited to see who would be the first to get laced up and skating on the ice. We played this game every day. As a matter of fact, I think my dad started the friendly competition, so we didn't waste time. The five of us took the "game" as a competitive challenge. Last year Colin and I were usually the first ones on the ice.

Dalton, our goalie, had more gear, so he was the last one every time.

I looked around the room as I pulled on my skates. Today Dalton was surprisingly fast and almost done. Colin was still trying to untie his skates from the last time he wore them, while Lucas and Nathan weren't even close to being ready.

My left foot slammed into my skate, and I started lacing as I hustled toward the exit door that led to the ice rink. I stumbled through the door as I was bending down trying to finish tying my skates. I had just finished tying them when I clumsily stumbled onto the ice where a large number of kids were already skating and warming up. As soon as I hit the ice, I turned back to see Nathan with Lucas following closely behind him.

"I gotcha both!" I exclaimed, laughing while watching both of them clumsily trying to beat each other to the ice. Nathan was already sweating, and I could tell Lucas was disappointed I had beat him.

My dream season was already off to a perfect start. I won bragging rights for that entire night and the next day at school. While my bragging rights didn't ease the pain of the English class foul up, it still felt good to be first.

I stood gloating with my back to the ice, watching as Nathan and Lucas came closer. Right before they reached the edge of the rink, both boys abruptly stopped and stared directly at me.

The look I saw on their face told me something was radically wrong, and I needed to turn around. They had the exact same expression on their face that they had in English class—a look of complete shock.

I turned back toward the ice and the mob of players skating around. For a split second, nothing really caught my attention. But as I scanned the rink, I saw my dad at the back of the ice rink talking to someone in full dress I couldn't identify from that distance.

I squinted and fixed my eyes on the player, blocking out all of the other kids warming up. I still couldn't see who it was, so I slowly skated toward my dad. Only then did I notice to whom he was talking.

I stopped skating. Nathan and Lucas, who had followed me across the ice, glided up beside me.

"Is that who I think it is?" asked Lucas.

"Tell me that is not the Bladebreaker," Nathan said behind me in an awe-inspired tone.

I couldn't believe my eyes. On our ice next to

my dad stood our greatest rival—our enemy. My dad was talking to Bobby "the Bladebreaker" Hall.

"Why in the world would he be here?" I said angrily out loud.

- 8 -

The Frozen Five had a long bitter history with the Bladebreaker, starting three years ago at a hockey tournament in Detroit.

Our Barn Burner team had made it to the championship finals one weekend and was pitted against our rivals, the Bay City Bears. It was the first time we had ever played the Bears in a tournament, which was surprising because theirs was one of the closest hockey clubs near us. They were only about an hour away from Bad Axe.

As soon as the game started, Bobby quickly made his presence known. The kid was super fast, and I don't mean like normal…I mean like a cheetah fast. He could zoom up and down the ice faster than I had ever seen any kid skate, including myself.

Thankfully, our team was better, and we were able to take a 4-2 lead heading into the last period. But Bobby made his presence felt the entire game by zooming and zigzagging intensely around the ice.

He also liked to chirp and talk trash to the opposing team. That was one lesson my dad had taught all of us early on—no trash talking or putting down the other team. Bobby's coach must have forgotten to have that conversation with him.

Every time he made a move or did something good, he would tell everyone about it. By the third period, I was sick of his snarky remarks and comments. He had scored his team's only two goals, and even though we were winning by two goals, I was frustrated. Because of Bobby's brashness, I felt like we were losing.

Little did I know, we hadn't seen anything yet. The third period horn blasted, announcing the start of the final period.

I had no idea that Bobby would do something that would make his name legendary across junior hockey leagues around the state.

The third period was intense, with an abundance of back-and-forth action on the ice.

With five minutes left, Bobby got the puck at center ice and raced toward our goals. Colin, one of our best defenders, raced backward to try to slow Bobby down. As they drew closer to the goal, Bobby went into hyperdrive, flipping into a whole new gear and flying faster than ever. He was racing down the right side, then suddenly stopped and crossed over to the left.

While that was a common move on the ice, nothing was ordinary about Bobby's move.

Bobby's move was so fast and agile that Colin was completely caught off guard. Knowing he was beat to his left, Colin slammed his skates into the ice.

When he planted, the blade on his left skate broke completely off, sending Colin flying onto the ice. Bobby took advantage of the misstep, glided past, and scored his third goal, cutting our lead to one, now 4-3.

The entire rink stood and stared as Colin had to get helped off the ice. One of our coaches walked over and picked up the broken blade from the ice. Bobby was celebrating and cheering with his team, as well as taunting Colin and making fun of him.

Still in shock from Bobby's amazing move, I skated back to center ice for a face-off after the goal. I knew I didn't want Bobby to embarrass me like he had Colin.

"Hey, kid," Bobby yelled toward me.

"Me?" I questioned.

"You're next," he said.

Anger started to well up deep inside my stomach as this kid continued to talk trash. When the puck was dropped, I forgot about the score and charged toward Bobby, checking him hard and knocking him on his back. His body crumpled and made a loud thud on the ice.

The referee blew his whistle and put me in the penalty box for 2:00 minutes of the last three minutes of the game. My display of anger gave Bobby and his team a power-play opportunity they promptly capitalized on. The Bay City Bears scored the tying goal with 43 seconds remaining.

Bay City had tied the game, and it was all my fault. Thankfully, we ended up winning 5-4 in double overtime. Dad was not happy that I had let my temper get the best of me. I knew I couldn't let that happen again.

The next day my dad showed me a newspaper article about the game. Along with a picture of Bobby, the sports editor had titled the event "The Bladebreaker Strikes Again" in big bold letters.

Looks like Bobby got a new nickname and a ton of notoriety at Colin's expense.

The newspaper story made Bobby seem like he was some kind of hero or something. He may have been a great hockey player, but I didn't like him.

Now here on our home ice stood the enemy having a casual conversation with my dad.

I snapped back into reality and skated toward them.

The Golden Puck

"What's this kid doing on my ice?" I said in a loud, aggressive tone that echoed around the rink.

All the other kids stopped skating to watch my interaction with my dad.

Dad stopped talking to Bobby and looked at me. His facial expression let me know right away that I was out of line for talking to him like that.

Bobby skated in the opposite direction to continue to warm up. I squinted, trying to read his jersey. Instead of having his last name, his hockey jersey said Bladebreaker on the back.

"This kid really thinks he is something," I said to myself.

His ego wasn't even the worst of it.

On the back of his jersey, I saw number 26 in big, bold numbers.

He's wearing my number!

- 9 -

Suddenly, the anticipated first day of practice paused, and I felt like everything was moving in slow motion. I stood my ground, staring toward Bobby.

"We will talk after practice," Dad said as nicely as he could.

"No, I want to talk now!" I said.

Dad spun toward me and shot me a look. At that point, I could tell Dad was seriously upset and it would be in my best interest to let the matter go until after practice.

Dad skated away, and as I was about to start warming up, out of the corner of my eye I saw a blur coming in my direction. I turned toward it.

The Golden Puck

"Bobby Hall," he said, taking off his right glove and extending his hand to shake mine. There was an awkward pause before I extended my hand back to him.

"I look forward to playing with you, Caleb. Now that I'm here, we are going to be unstoppable!" he said as he smiled and turned to skate back toward center ice.

He didn't even give me time to reply. He doesn't seem too interested in hearing from me.

"What did I miss?" Dalton asked as he walked toward me. "Is it me, or did that kid look like the Bladebreaker?"

"That's him, no doubt," said Lucas.

"What is my dad thinking?" I said, skating away from the group. I shifted weight quickly and picked up my speed as I raced to the back corner of the rink where Dad was working with some kids on footwork drills.

"Dad, you got a second? Can I chat with you?" I asked.

"Right now?" Dad questioned. "I think it would

be best if we talked on the way home, Caleb." He was obviously trying to nicely drop a hint for me to stop talking about it. He didn't like being interrupted when he was coaching and working with kids on the ice.

"Yeah, please," I said with a sense of urgency.

He stopped and told the kids to keep skating. Dad could tell that I wasn't going to go away.

"Listen. First of all, I didn't know he was coming until he showed up today. If I did, I would have told you so you could have been prepared," Dad said.

"You're not going to let *him* on our team, are you?" I asked.

"*Let* him on the team? This is called a tryout, Caleb. That means anyone can try out for our travel team. You and I both know he is a great hockey player. Why wouldn't we welcome him on our team?" Dad asked.

"He's the Bladebreaker, Dad! Do I need to remind you? He is not a team player; he won't fit in with us," I said.

"Son, you don't know that. He gets a fair chance like everyone else," said Dad.

"What about his Bay City team? Why doesn't he just go back and play with them again? They probably don't want to have to deal with him either."

"That's not my place to talk about that. I will let him tell you about that if he wants to," said Dad.

"This kid shows up, and now he is on our team? Bobby's a Barn Burner?" I asked in a pleading voice, hoping he would say something otherwise.

"Caleb, this is about a team—not a single player. We will give him a chance. You need to talk to your buddies and make him feel accepted," Dad said.

I was so angry and frustrated I didn't know what to do. The only thing that crossed my mind was to skate away before I said something to my father I would later regret.

- 10 -

Besides Bobby showing up, tryouts went exactly as I thought they would. The core of our team was back, and we added the great Bladebreaker.

In the locker room after practice, I sat quietly thinking. Everyone else was taking off their stuff, but I just sat in deep thought. A lot of emotions were running through my mind, and I wasn't sure how to respond next.

Bobby was the first one out of the locker room. He didn't speak to anyone, just grabbed his stuff and zoomed out.

For a guy joining a new team, he sure doesn't act like he wants to be a great teammate. He didn't even talk to a single player.

The Golden Puck

I waited in the locker room until only the Frozen Five were left.

"I can't believe this," I finally said, slamming my helmet against my locker. The sound startled Dalton who was sitting next to me.

"Totally not what I was expecting about tryouts when I woke up this morning," said Nathan.

We went around the room complaining or saying something negative about the day. Dalton went back to his slipup in English class. Colin and Nathan were not happy the Bladebreaker was there.

"What are you thinking, Lucas?" I asked.

"I'm thinking maybe we are looking at this situation all wrong," he said.

"How else do you want us to look at it?" I asked.

"Well, I mean our main team goal is to win. We knew we would be a really good hockey team. Now with Bobby, we are an even better team," said Lucas. He added, "Everything we have talked about for the past couple of years is still a good possibility. He does make us better for the Golden Puck Tournament next month."

For a couple minutes, we sat quietly, and I thought about what both Dad and Lucas had said. *Am I upset that we're adding a star hockey player? Am I thinking about winning or about having some of the attention taken off me?* The more I thought about it, the more I realized that I was really thinking of how his presence would affect me. I had to admit he would make our team a lot better.

"Let's give the kid a chance," said Dalton.

"All those in favor," said Lucas.

Four loud "yes" votes rang through the locker room. One rule of the Frozen Five was to vote on any big decisions, and the majority of the votes always won.

"No! Sorry, but I don't like the kid," I said.

"The vote was placed; sorry, Caleb. You know the rules: the majority always wins," said Lucas.

We took off the rest of our stuff as Dad and the other coaches walked into the locker room. There was no talk of Bobby or anything else. I cleaned up our gear and threw it into our heavy travel hockey bags.

The Golden Puck

"All right, boys, I will see you guys tomorrow in school," I said, walking out. I turned and added, "At least we only have to deal with the Bladebreaker for a couple hours at practice."

Driving home in the car, I didn't say a word to Dad. He knew I wasn't happy, and I knew that he was upset about how I was acting toward Bobby joining our team.

Our car made a noisy crunching sound as we turned onto our gravel road. Dad drove the mile down our road before pulling into the driveway and shutting off the car.

"Thanks for the ride," I finally said.

"Caleb, I know things aren't starting the way you had hoped, but that doesn't mean this won't be a great year," Dad said.

I managed a half smile, half smirk. "Well, it can't get much worse," I said, slamming the door more forcefully than normal.

I went inside, showered, and went straight to my room. I rested in bed as I listened to music before falling into a deep sleep.

- 11 -

The next morning I woke up and saw a huge smear of drool on my pillow. My music was still playing. I had been so tired I had forgotten to shut it off. It took me a couple minutes to realize where I was and what day it was. I had gotten a solid night's sleep. My body felt refreshed from the long night's slumber.

I stumbled out to the kitchen and poured a bowl of cereal. Dad was up early and already at work. Mom greeted me with a hug and smile.

"How is school going?" Mom asked in a gentle tone.

Whenever my mom was digging for answers, her voice became low and overly sweet.

The Golden Puck

"Fine," I said, chomping on my cereal.

"Okay, not trying to pry. Just wondering," she said softly.

"School is fine, Mom. Hockey stinks," I said, realizing I was being rude.

"Really, after only one day?" Mom said in a questioning tone.

"Mom, I know Dad told you about Bobby," I said.

"He did," Mom said. She quickly added, "Maybe this could be good, Caleb."

"I don't like him; I have never liked him. He won't fit in with our team," I quickly snapped.

"You might be right, Caleb…but there is a chance you could be totally wrong too. Didn't you say he was a great player?" Mom asked.

"He's pretty good, but I don't think I would call him great," I said.

I quickly asked, "What's your point? So what if he's good. Does that make how he acts better or worse?"

Mom thought for a second. She was trying to choose the right words before speaking.

"Caleb, may I ask you just one more question?" she said politely. "Then I promise I will leave you alone and let you enjoy breakfast."

"Sure, Mom," I said.

"Does he make your team better?" she asked.

I went to answer quickly then caught myself. I drew in a deep breath and really considered her question.

After a couple seconds of silence, I answered, "Yes, he does make our team better."

"May I ask you one more question, Son?" she said again.

"Yes," I said, starting to get annoyed with my mom being right.

"What is your ultimate goal this year?" she asked.

"To be the best. I want everyone to know that I am the best hockey player in Huron County," I said.

"Shouldn't your goal be something that is centered around the team?" she asked.

I instantly shot out an answer. I didn't need time to think about it; I knew what the biggest goal for our team was.

The Golden Puck

"That would be to win the Golden Puck," I said.

"Does adding Bobby help that goal or make it harder?" she asked.

I didn't need to answer; I got her point. I walked over and kissed her on the top of her head.

"Thanks for the talk, Mom," I said.

My mom always had a way of connecting with me, showing me a way to look at things differently. Dad was always super intense, and Mom was always patient and calm.

"Have a great day at school," she said.

I turned, walking out the front door and down the steps. At the bottom of the steps, I heard Mom calling my name, so I turned to watch her hurrying to the front door.

"I almost forgot! Your dad left you this note this morning. He wanted you to read it before school," she said.

"Thanks," I said, slipping the note into my right pants pocket. I had to jog to catch the bus and momentarily forgot about the note as I climbed the bus steps. Plus, the last thing I wanted was a bunch of high schoolers seeing me read a note from my parents on the bus.

I sat quietly on the bus, staring out the window. *One thing Mom was right about: Bobby did make our team way better.*

Maybe I could put up with him for a couple hours at hockey practice.

- 12 -

Our bus was running behind that day because our last stop was at Tommy Thompson's house. Tommy, a tenth grader, was still sleeping when we arrived at his house.

Mr. Reynolds, our bus driver, hit the horn three times before Tommy came running, eating toast and swinging a black backpack. Obviously, the bus driver's horn woke him up.

His tardiness delayed the bus by almost ten minutes. By the time we walked into school, the first bell had already rung. Kids were sitting in their first-hour class.

I jogged to my locker and grabbed my math book before heading to Mr. Jones' classroom.

I walked in and immediately apologized to Mr. Jones for being late.

"It's okay, Caleb. I heard about the bus. Please take your seat," said Mr. Jones.

I turned to walk toward my usual seat in the back of the class but noticed someone was already sitting in it. Everyone in the entire school knew that was my seat.

As I got closer, I couldn't believe my eyes. Sitting in my seat was the Bladebreaker!

I quickly looked at Dalton and Colin who were sitting next to the Bladebreaker. They were staring at me, just as surprised as I was.

"Caleb, please find a seat," Mr. Jones said in a polite but firm tone. I could feel the entire class watching to see what I would do.

Bladebreaker sat there smiling at me with a smug, sarcastic look on his face. My first thought was to walk over and shove him out of my seat to show everyone in the school that the Frozen Five don't play around. Luckily, I knew that wasn't the right choice.

The Golden Puck

I walked to the back corner and sat in the only empty seat left in the classroom.

Mr. Jones started his lesson, and I reached in my pocket to grab a pencil for notes. I felt the piece of paper Mom had given me during breakfast. I had forgotten about it and was surprised when I felt it. I pulled it out and opened my math textbook to hide the note as I unfolded it.

Caleb,
   Things will get better, and we are going to have an awesome hockey season. I wanted to tell you that Bobby is not just going to be on the hockey team. His family moved into Bad Axe, so you will see him at school today. I didn't want you to be surprised. I love you, Son.
Dad

"Why didn't I read my dad's note on the bus?" I asked myself, knowing that it would have saved me the embarrassment of finding Bobby in my math class. *Dad knew I would be upset seeing Bobby at school. He was trying to give me a heads up to avoid more drama.*

I groaned inwardly. *I should have read the note as soon as Mom handed it to me.*

I didn't know it at the time, but things were about to change in my life, and I would need my dad's wisdom and encouragement more than ever!

- 13 -

Lunch, my favorite part of the school day, was a time for the Frozen Five to talk. Usually our conversation was about hockey, but we also talked about classes and girls.

Everyone knew that the five of us sat together at the third table on the right side of the lunchroom. In our lunchroom, every table was spoken for by one group or another. The cheerleaders, the football players, and even the chess kids had their own table.

The entire school was comfortable with this routine and pattern. Several open tables near the salad bar were open for anyone who wanted to sit there.

The Frozen Five had their own table, and it was important that we did. Lucas had gym class right next to the cafeteria, so he was always one of the first ones in the lunchroom. He secured our table—the same one every year and the same five people every year. It had been that way since the fifth grade.

"What in the world is Bobby doing here?" Dalton asked.

"I guess his family has moved into Bad Axe," I said.

"Man, I can't get away from that kid. I still have nightmares about…well, you know," said Colin.

"He does have a great slap shot though," said Lucas.

I turned and gave him a nasty look.

"I mean, he is good; you know that, Caleb," said Lucas.

"I'll admit that he's good," I said.

"Maybe he isn't all that bad. Let's give him a chance," said Dalton.

Before I had time to say anything, I saw a con-

The Golden Puck

cerned look on Lucas's face. I turned around to look behind me to see what he was staring at.

Our whole table turned toward the condiment station at the end of the lunch line. Bobby was leaning against the wall, looking calm and confident. His smooth demeanor was shocking when we saw that he was talking to Kelly.

There wasn't an eighth-grade boy in the school who didn't have a crush on Kelly Markowski. I tried to talk to her once, and it was disastrous. I started stumbling and tripping over my words. Speechless, I quickly left.

The Bladebreaker stood confidently laughing, and Kelly even started twirling her hair.

This kid... I thought to myself.

We stared in amazement as he held a couple-minute conversation with Kelly. We did the only thing we could do: we stared in awe that the Bladebreaker was talking to her.

Suddenly, Bobby looked past Kelly and toward our table. He knew we were staring in awe at his performance and shot us a quick, confident wink.

"Wow…what can this kid not do?" asked Nathan.

It seemed like Bobby was doing everything in his power to aggravate me. My dislike for him kept growing and growing.

Finally, Kelly walked off toward the cheerleaders' table. Bobby started walking, a confident strut, toward our table.

"How's it going, fellas? Got room for a sixth?" he asked, sounding like some Hollywood movie star.

"No worries; you can have my seat," I said rudely as I got up. Our shoulders briefly bumped, but I never looked back.

Walking to class, I came to a frightening conclusion. The Bladebreaker wasn't here just to take over my hockey team. He was on a mission to take everything—my school, my seat, Kelly, and even my best friends.

I wasn't about to turn everything over to him that easily. Bladebreaker was about to see a whole different side of me—one he wasn't going to like.

The Golden Puck

There might be room on our Barn Burner hockey team, but there wasn't room in the Frozen Five for a sixth person, especially the Bladebreaker.

- 14 -

I was glad this was the second and last day of tryouts. Actual hockey practice couldn't come fast enough. I knew Bladebreaker was going to be on our team, and today at practice I planned on showing him why I was the starting center and leading scorer.

Hockey tryouts were split between various drills and activities that allowed us to showcase our skills for all the coaches. They evaluated our skating speed, our puck handling, and other hockey-related skills.

After two hours of intense training and drills, I was glad when my dad finally blew the whistle signaling us to join him at center ice.

The Golden Puck

"I want to thank you all for trying out. Remember, if you don't make the team this year, don't quit on yourself. Keep working and try out again next year," Dad said, looking over all the eager eyes. It was a big deal to make our team, and I was proud to be on it.

"If I call your name," Dad continued, "please stay so I can go over team practices and rules."

One by one he started calling off names, the Frozen Five and Bladebreaker. He announced fifteen names, and the other twenty or so hopeful players left with lowered heads.

"For those of you who made it, congratulations. You earned your slot. But also keep in mind twenty kids are leaving the rink right now who would love to be in your skates. Value being a member of this team!" Dad declared enthusiastically.

For the next twenty minutes, Dad went over our upcoming practice and game schedule, handing out a packet of information that included our calendar with all the events listed for the season. He went through each event, starting with our first big tournament, the Turkey Classic, which always took place the weekend before Thanksgiving.

That means we have less than three weeks to prepare.

He then addressed the Golden Puck Tournament. Just hearing the words "Golden Puck" sent chills down my spine. I had wanted to play and win that tournament ever since I started playing peewee hockey as a four-year-old.

"I know I don't need to tell you guys this, but the Golden Puck Tournament in Calumet is less than a month away. That's a big one, boys, but I don't want to talk about it yet; we have a long season ahead," Dad said.

To be ready, the next couple weeks we would practice five days per week right after school until five-thirty in the evening. The excitement on everyone's face was clear and encouraging.

"One more thing before we end today," Dad said. "I was going over your registration forms, and it appears we have a conflict with two players wanting the same number."

The Golden Puck

I looked around at all the new players on the team. Most of them had been local kids who bounced back and forth between our team and the second team.

"Just to be fair, I want to remind everyone what the protocol is when two players want to wear the same number," he said.

I knew the protocol; I guessed that all the kids knew what had to happen. It would come down to an old-fashioned shootout. I smiled just thinking about watching it. All I could think about was who the two lucky ones were who would have to fight for their number.

The tradition with the Barn Burners was simple. Whenever two players wanted the same number, a five-shot shootout was called. Whoever made the most shots out of five went home with his choice of the jersey number.

It had only happened one other time during my hockey career.

I smiled, looking around and wondering who it would be.

"I need Caleb and Bobby to grab their sticks and meet me at the blueline. As you know, only one player can wear number 26," Dad announced.

- 15 -

The Bladebreaker is trying to take everything I love from me.

My dream hockey season was quickly becoming a nightmare. Now I had to do a shootout with Bobby to even get my number—the same number I had worn since I started playing hockey.

I had been number 26 from the beginning. It was my number, and I wasn't going to let Bobby take anything else from me.

Even though practice was over, no one left. All the players remained, kneeling on the ice. They all wanted to see what was going to happen with my showdown with the Bladebreaker.

Lots of thoughts ran through my mind. *Why*

didn't Dad just tell Bobby to choose another number? I'm his son; twenty-six is my number.

One thing about my dad: he approached coaching hockey the same way he approached life. He always did the right thing—not the convenient or best thing for himself—but the right thing.

As I skated to the blue line, I knew Dad was following the rules. My dad coached all of us hard but none harder than me. At first, I didn't like it or understand why.

After my first season, what he asked of me made sense. My dad knew how good I could be, and he pushed me toward that level of hockey. He was trying to help me reach my potential. I wanted to be coached, and I wanted to be pushed.

All my years of playing hockey have taught me that a coach's duty is to push and get the most out of his players. My dad was an expert at it. I didn't get offended; in fact, I was more concerned if he wasn't pushing me. I knew if he was taking the time to coach and correct me, he wanted me to be the best hockey player I could be.

The Golden Puck

Here I was, following our team rules in a shoot-out with Bobby to see who could wear the number 26 jersey for the season.

A number seemingly takes on an identity of its own, and a player becomes part of that identity. A jersey number has a much deeper meaning for the player wearing it. Sometimes a number represents a special day or is the one their dad or brother wore. For me, it was much simpler.

Growing up, my dad loved baseball. His true passion was cheering on the Boston Red Sox. One of my earliest memories was walking into my dad's home office and seeing a framed, autographed number 26 Boston Red Sox jersey hanging on the wall. Wade Boggs had played eighteen seasons with the Boston Red Sox before spending four years with the New York Yankees. During that time, Boggs was a twelve-time all-star, eight-time Silver Slugger, and a two-time Gold Glove winner.

The funny thing is, I didn't know who Wade Boggs was, nor did I even like baseball. I knew that jersey was special and meant something to my dad.

I would walk into his office and stare at it, admiring the autograph. Dad loved that jersey.

I knew number 26 was special to my dad, so it became special to me. During my first hockey season when my dad asked me what number I wanted, I didn't hesitate. Number 26 was not just a number or a jersey that I wore; it became part of me.

For the past five seasons, I had worn number 26 with great pride. I was known as number 26; all my hoodies and club shirts had the number on it.

I was number 26.

-16-

Dad had set five pucks on the blue line in two spots. There was no goalie, just the open ice and the goalie net.

The distance from the blue line to the empty net is about sixty-four feet. A lot can happen to a hockey puck traveling that distance on the ice.

I shot first. My arms tensed, and I pulled back and blasted a hard slap shot toward the goal. As the puck traveled, it looked like it was going to go wide right. I watched in horror as the roughed-up ice pulled the puck, but at the last minute, the puck hit the side of the goal post and ricocheted into the net, 1-0 in favor of me…

Bobby shot, and his puck sailed wide left—a

clear miss. For my second shot, I tried to repeat everything I had done on the first. Unfortunately, I took a little power off as I tried to aim and missed badly to the right.

Bobby made his second shot.

I missed my third.

Bobby made his third shot.

I made my fourth, and the Bladebreaker missed.

We were tied at 2-2 apiece with one shot left. Now the entire hockey rink had stopped to watch our contest.

It was so quiet I could hear my stick hit the ice as I approached for my last shot.

"You better make this. No pressure, but I know that I'm going to make it," Bobby said, looking in my direction. The sound of his voice made me so mad. I could feel my heart beating and blood running through my veins.

I reared back with my stick and smashed the puck as hard as I could. The Bladebreaker had gotten into my head one more time. Instead of aiming and taking my time, I went with the power shot.

The Golden Puck

It didn't work. My shot flew wide right before smashing into boards with a loud thud. I heard a hush come over the crowd.

Bobby stood tall over his puck and turned toward me, grinning. I had been so frustrated that I choked and missed the shot.

With ease, the Bladebreaker drew back and dropped a perfect shot from the blue line that split straight down the ice. As soon as he hit it, I knew it was good.

His shot landed dead center in the middle of the net.

I lost 3-2.

Dad tried saying something to me, but I ignored him as I skated toward the locker room. I couldn't even think about playing hockey and not wearing the number 26 jersey.

I started ripping at my skates to untie them. I wanted to cry so badly, it took every bit of me not to. I was mad, frustrated, and disappointed in myself all at the same time.

When the players entered, Dalton came up to

me and patted me on the back. "I am sorry, Caleb," he said.

I kept untying my skates without looking up. Slowly one by one, my teammates entered. Most of them kept their distance. When the locker room was almost empty, Lucas came and sat by me.

"That's a bummer," he said softly. I knew my friends were trying to make me feel better. Nothing they could have said at that moment would have helped.

It wasn't just about the jersey; I felt like I was losing everything I loved about hockey. I would have to choose another number and share the ice with some hotshot kid.

Bobby walked in, sensed my frustration, and changed, leaving without saying a word.

After changing, I grabbed my bag and headed to my dad's car. I got in and locked the doors. I felt a slight ease in my pain for the first time now that I was alone.

Ten minutes later, Dad walked out. I unlocked the doors without ever looking up. He patted me on the head. "Caleb, there is nothing I can say to take your pain away. Sometimes life just isn't fair," he said.

We pulled out of the hockey arena, and as I stared out the window, I couldn't help but feel sorry for myself.

"Sometimes life just isn't fair," I kept repeating to myself. *That's the best speech my dad could give me at this moment?* His words echoed through my mind, leaving a lasting imprint on my soul.

- 17 -

Over the next two weeks, I stayed out of certain areas around school. I was embarrassed and needed time to recover. I still talked to the Frozen Five, although the jersey shootout never came up again.

They had known me long enough to know when to leave a subject alone.

I avoided the Bladebreaker.

He had tried talking to me several times in the hallway, but I just ignored him, walking away. His arrogant attitude drove me crazy. There was a hint of jealousy that made his words bother me even more. This guy moved to *my* school, joined *my* team, talked to the girl I had a crush on forever, and took *my* number.

The Golden Puck

There was nothing I wanted to hear from him.

At practice, we coexisted. I knew my job was to help our team win, so when we were on the ice, I tried to treat him like all my other teammates.

I played center, and he played right wing.

The Bladebreaker could definitely play hockey; his skating skills were top-notch and better than anyone on the team. I could handle the puck better, but when it came to skating, I couldn't touch him.

Dad never brought up the jersey number again, but when the uniforms came in, he tossed me number 27. I took it without saying a word. I guess he figured it was as close to number 26 as I could get.

Finally, it was time for our new team to play in our first tournament. When the puck dropped, it was apparent that ours was a totally different team.

The addition of the Bladebreaker took us to a whole new level as a team.

In our first game, we won 5-2, and I scored two goals. The game was never close as we took a 4-0 lead into the third period. Adding another score took a lot of pressure off Dalton, our goalie.

We controlled the puck most of the game, and the puck seldom made it into our defensive zone.

The second game had the same results, and we won 4-1, dominating the entire game.

Our team easily made it to the finals, and the Barn Burners were slated to play a good team from Minnesota.

Before the game, a younger kid came up to me and said, "You're a really good player."

I smiled, embarrassed. I didn't know what to say as the kid stood there staring at me.

"Thanks," I finally muttered.

"Can you sign this puck for me? My dad said that you are so good you are going to be a professional hockey player someday," he said.

I grinned sheepishly and smiled awkwardly. I wasn't good at getting compliments.

I did feel pretty proud that this little hockey player was looking up to me and that his dad thought I was good enough to be a pro player.

I grabbed the silver marker from his hand as he handed me a black hockey puck.

The Golden Puck

I signed number 27 Caleb Geiger on the puck and handed it back to him.

The little boy had such an excited look on his face as he stared at the puck. His expression reminded me of the way that I had looked at my dad's Wade Bogg jersey in his office.

Suddenly his expression changed from joy to confusion.

He looked at me then back at the puck.

"What's wrong, little buddy?" I asked, wondering if I signed it in the wrong spot or if the signature had smeared.

"You're number 27?" he asked, puzzled.

"Yeah," I said, confused.

"Oh…thanks," he said in a long tone.

He added, "I thought you were number 26." The kid walked away disappointed. My feelings of pride quickly drained.

The young boy didn't want my autograph. His dad didn't think I was going to be a pro.

They want the Bladebreaker.

- 18 -

A big crowd had gathered as we took the ice against the Minneapolis Blizzard. I hadn't told anyone about the autograph incident.

My negative feelings toward Bobby continued to spiral, and I was determined to have the best game I had ever had. I was going to show that kid who wanted my autograph and his dad who the real future pro was.

A highly skilled hockey team, the Blizzard players were big and fast. I had seen them play once at a tournament last year in Columbus, Ohio. Not surprisingly, they had won the tournament.

Before the season, I would have never put our team in the same category as the Blizzards. But now, after the addition of the Bladebreaker, the Barn Burners were playing at a comparable level.

Being in front of all those people was exciting. The championship game on Sunday always has the most spectators, and the energy in the building was hard to ignore.

The first period was slow, with both teams trying to feel out their opponent. I had one breakaway shot but was stonewalled by the Blizzard's goalie. I shot a slapshot high into the net, and the goalie made an amazing glove save.

At the end of the first period, we were both scoreless, 0-0.

The second period started off with a bang. The Bladebreaker stole the puck at center ice and raced toward their goalie. As he neared the goalie and a defenseman, Bobby performed a quick deke by positioning the puck smoothly between his legs. The move faked out the goalie and defenseman, and Bobby backhanded the puck in for a goal. This high-level play gave us a 1-0 lead. It looked like we were going to go into intermission with the lead before tragedy struck with :30 remaining in the period.

A Blizzard's defender swiped the puck away from me and passed ahead to his left wing. Knowing there wasn't much time on the clock, the wing steadied the puck and fired a high shot toward the net. The quick shot caught Dalton off guard, and he was slow to react. By the time Dalton lunged toward the puck, it was too late. We were now in a tie game, 1-1. The buzzer sounded, and we headed into the locker room with our heads low.

We shouldn't have given up that goal. It wasn't Dalton's fault; it started with my lazy puck handling. After a short rest and a strategy session on the bench, we skated out for the third and final period.

In the back of my mind, I knew how important this tournament was. Even though it was our first of the season, it could set the tone for the rest of the year. Winning this tournament against the Blizzards would be a huge confidence booster for our entire team.

A couple minutes into the third period, I stole

The Golden Puck

the puck and had a one-on-one breakaway with the goalie. It was just the two of us, and this time I took advantage, scoring on a wrist shot.

The goal gave us a 2-1 lead with 7:14 left in the game. I knew all we had to do was play aggressively, take care of the puck, and we would be crowned champions.

The next six and a half minutes were filled with masterful puck handling by the Barn Burners. Bobby and I took over the game, kept the puck away from the Blizzard offense, and took time off the clock.

With under a minute left, I flipped the puck to Colin who was sitting out wide on the left wing. Colin went to pass the puck back to me. As he started to pass, he lost his footing on the ice. He stumbled, and the puck ricocheted off his skates toward our goal.

The play unfolded in slow motion. I stood off guard as a Blizzard player scooped up the puck with his stick and raced toward Dalton, who had been left alone in the goal.

Seconds later the horn blasted, a Blizzard goal. The game was tied 2-2 with fifteen seconds left in the third period.

-19-

All the hard work and great hockey, but one simple mistake gave the Blizzards the opportunity to tie the game.

As I skated to center ice, I looked to my right to see Bobby with his stick down ready. He had a look on his face that said *I'm confident we can still score.* Something behind the Bladebreaker caught my attention. I squinted through sweaty eyes to see the young kid who had asked for the autograph. He was standing next to his dad in the front row cheering.

I'm going to show this kid who the real star on the ice is!

I carefully settled my stick down on the ice for

the face-off. I knew if we had any chance to win the game in regulation, I had to win this face-off.

"Caleb," I heard Bobby yelling just as the referee was about to drop the puck. I glanced and noticed the defenseman was too far up, and Bobby had a huge advantage. He was signaling for me to pass the puck up the ice, and he would be open. I saw it and quickly realized Bobby was right. He would be open.

Then I made a split-second decision.

I'm not going to pass the puck to Bobby. Even though it was the right play and a play that might help us win the game, I was going to fake it to Bobby and blast the puck up the ice to myself.

The puck hit the ice with a loud thud, and I maneuvered my stick toward Bobby then back toward the middle of the ice. I hit the puck perfectly between the Blizzard center and raced down the ice.

The clock ticked as I raced toward the goalie. I wound up and took a deep slap shot from center ice.

I was too far away and watched as the puck lost

The Golden Puck

velocity as it skidded toward the net. It was obvious that the shot wasn't even going to make it to the goalie in time.

Just as I was about to give up hope, I saw a blur out of the corner of my eye and recognized the Bladebreaker racing down the ice. He intercepted the puck a couple of feet in front of the net, deflecting the puck. The puck shot off Bobby's stick. The goalie dove toward the right side of the net, and the puck disappeared.

At first, I thought the goalie had landed on it.

Suddenly a horn blasted, and a red light swirled behind the goalie, signaling a goal.

The buzzer sounded, and the Barn Burners won 3-2.

In all the excitement of winning, I had forgotten about my selfish play. Most people watching wouldn't have known; they might have even thought I passed it toward the net to the Bladebreaker.

Our team rushed the ice and mobbed each other. After a couple minutes, Dad walked out with a huge trophy, and we took pictures at center ice. I made eye contact with Bobby, who was staring at me with a weird look on his face.

I quickly looked away, knowing why he was eyeballing me. Bobby knew the truth that I had decided not to pass him the puck. Dad and I posed kissing the trophy on the ice before skating into the locker room.

Inside the locker room was a party. Kids were hugging and laughing, proud to be tournament champions.

Beating the Blizzards was a big deal and exciting.

The amazing feeling of winning didn't last long.

Next week would prove to be the worst week of my life.

- 20 -

Monday mornings are usually tough on me. We didn't get home from the tournament until late on Sunday night, and I was exhausted.

I hit the snooze button at least ten times before Mom finally came and pulled the covers off.

"Caleb, you have to get up, or you're going to be late for school!" she yelled as the cold air hit my legs.

I jumped up, unaware that it was even morning. I was so tired, I was confused about what day it was. When I finally got my bearings, I remembered it was Monday morning.

I hustled into school still wiping the sleep out of my eyes. I only had a couple minutes before the first bell rang. I jogged my way toward the cafeteria to grab breakfast.

When I entered the cafeteria, kids started clapping and cheering. I was surprised at first then glanced over at a smiling table full of our hockey players. I walked over.

"Pretty cool, huh," said Nathan.

"Yeah, not bad at all," I said smiling.

"All this for us," I asked.

"Yep, I sure am enjoying it," said Dalton.

As we were talking, a louder cheer came from behind me, and the entire place erupted. I turned toward the door to see Bobby.

They had erupted for the hero of the game. He strolled in with Kelly next to him. He had the game winner and the girl; the Bladebreaker was pretty much perfect in the eyes of everyone at Bad Axe Middle School.

"Here comes the hero," I said sarcastically.

"He did make an awesome goal," said Colin.

"But you were the one who passed him the puck," Lucas added.

The Golden Puck

His words stung, making the situation even worse. Deep down I knew that my selfishness had almost cost us the championship.

Just when I thought things couldn't get worse, they did.

A loud cheer started at the back of the cafeteria but eventually took over the whole place. When I first heard it, I got excited.

"Number 26, number 26," they chanted loudly.

For a split second, I forgot that Bobby had stolen my number, and I thought the cheers were for me. I turned to see the Bladebreaker waving to the crowd and kids offering him their orange juice.

As we left the cafeteria, I made up my mind. I had to do something about Bobby.

He was taking everything I loved, and he sure seemed to be enjoying it. *I have to come up with a plan, but what can I do? How can I fix this situation?*

Colin was the one who gave me the idea. I walked into math class, and the guys were talking about school.

"We start flag football today in gym class," Colin said.

"I know; I can't wait. Next to floor hockey, it's my favorite unit in gym," said Dalton.

The fall weather in Michigan is beautiful. Mr. Fields, our gym teacher, always has us play a three-week flag football unit that ends the week of Thanksgiving.

That's it! I will take care of Bobby on the football field, I thought to myself.

-21-

Mr. Fields always divided his teams evenly so no one had a stacked team with all the athletes. Since Bobby and I were two of the fastest kids in the entire school, I knew we wouldn't be on the same team.

As he announced the teams, I was happy that Colin was on my team. He was the only member of the Frozen Five on my team but having at least one close friend was still nice. Our class had seven teams of six kids.

My team was set to play Bobby's team during the second game today.

We won our first game easily, 42-18. I threw for a touchdown and ran for two. I enjoyed playing football but knew it would interfere with travel hockey, so I didn't play on our school team.

Bobby had a decent team, but overall, our team was way better. I knew the quarterback would try to pass Bobby the ball deep because he was so fast.

Our game plan was simple. Colin would guard Bobby up tight, and I would play deep on him so he couldn't beat us for a long pass. The plan was working to perfection, and we were leading 18-6 at halftime.

Bobby was starting to get frustrated, and I saw him arguing with his other teammates about not getting him the ball.

That's when I knew the perfect time to put my plan in motion had arrived.

Bobby's team had the ball first after halftime. On the first series, I dropped back to my usual spot. Only this time, I told Colin, "Once the ball is snapped, run deep. I will fly up and guard Bobby in case of a short pass."

Colin didn't know my entire plan though. As I came running up while Bobby was still running

The Golden Puck

and not looking in my direction, I ran into him as hard as I could.

I took out all of my frustration, jealousy, and anger in that one hit. I heard a loud thud as both of us tumbled to the ground. Bobby was slow to get up, and I was a little dazed.

Mr. Fields ran over. "Caleb, what in the world are you doing? You know you can't tackle in flag football!" he said in a furious tone.

It took Bobby a second to catch his breath, but once he got to his feet, he took off toward me.

He was covered in mud and grass.

I was ready for him and braced myself for a fight. I was tired of this new kid and didn't know what else was left to do.

As Bobby closed the distance, I felt Dalton's big arms close around me. His thick hands wrapped me up tight, and at the same time, Nathan grabbed Bobby from behind.

Luckily, the two intervened before a fistfight started.

Mr. Fields walked us both to the principal's

office, lecturing the whole way about good sportsmanship.

I was filled with such anger and rage. Bobby was looking at me, his disappointment obvious. He didn't seem angry at all, which surprised me. I know I would have been upset if someone had blindsided me.

We were both marched right into Mrs. Lewis's office.

Mr. Fields explained what happened as Mrs. Lewis's eyes widened.

Puzzled, she asked, "Aren't you boys on the same hockey team?"

Bobby nodded. I didn't say anything. For me to act that way was so out of character, and Mrs. Lewis noticed.

"Bobby, why don't you sit down in the office waiting room. I would like to talk to Caleb," she said softly.

Bobby stood and walked toward her office door. Mrs. Lewis quickly added, "Oh, honey, please shut the door behind you."

- 22 -

I respected Mrs. Lewis and enjoyed a great relationship with her. She was a kind, energetic person who always made me feel like she loved her job. I knew her well, especially after serving as the class president last year. We had enjoyed lots of talks and meetings together. My emotions changed to sadness when I saw I had disappointed her.

She sat quietly for a minute, staring out her window without saying a word. As I waited for her to speak, I could feel the tension leaving my body.

"Caleb, are you okay?" she finally asked in a sympathetic tone. I was expecting her to yell at me or to tell me how disappointed she was. When she didn't, she caught me off guard.

She leaned closer, looked me square in my eyes, and asked again, "Caleb, are you okay?" I could see the concern and honesty in her eyes.

My eyes began to well up; I couldn't hold back my feelings anymore. I started to cry, which was something I rarely did.

"What's really going on, honey?" she asked. I felt like Mrs. Lewis was the first person in the past month who really wanted to know how I was feeling.

I broke down completely as she handed me a tissue.

"It's Bobby; I hate him!" I barked.

As soon as I spoke, I regretted my words. My parents had always taught me that hating someone is wrong.

I could tell Mrs. Lewis was shocked. I was usually a calm, quiet kid. This was the first time I had ever been personally escorted to the principal's office by a teacher.

This visit was far different from the times I had received awards or had meetings with her.

The Golden Puck

She sat back and tapped her chin. I could tell she was thinking and making sure she said the right words.

"Hate is a strong word, Caleb," she said.

She's right; it is. However, I was so hurt and frustrated, I didn't know what else to say.

For the next forty-five minutes, I explained everything—all that I felt I had lost—to Mrs. Lewis. She sat quietly and listened. When I was finished, she sat back in her chair and looked out the window.

When she finally turned to me, she asked, "I don't think you really hate Bobby, do you?"

"No, ma'am," I said. I knew I didn't; I really liked and admired certain aspects of Bobby.

"It sounds like his arrival at our school has meant a big change for you. Sometimes change can be hard, and people handle it in different ways," said Mrs. Lewis.

"Yes, it's just been so hard," I agreed.

"I can see why. But how you handle change reflects on you," she said.

As I sat in Mrs. Lewis's office, considering her words, I started to think about everything that had happened. I realized that Bobby didn't deserve what I had done or how I had been acting.

"Well, Caleb, I need to call your parents. Some type of discipline is required; we can't have boys knocking each other around, almost fighting at our school," she said.

"Okay," I said, standing. I knew my parents were going to be disappointed. My dad would especially be upset upon hearing what I had done.

I walked out and sat down. Bobby got up without looking at me. As he walked in, I noticed his pants were grass-stained and his shirt had a big rip in it.

I felt terrible, knowing that hammering him in the flag football game had been wrong.

Now I had to deal with the consequences of my bad decision. I knew I would be in big trouble once I got home, but I was hoping that Mrs. Lewis wouldn't suspend me from school.

My perfect school discipline record I had

worked so hard to keep unblemished was about to be ruined. I felt sure Mrs. Lewis was going to suspend me. *How long will it be? Three days? Five days? It doesn't matter. Seems like no matter what I do, my days and weeks just keep getting worse and worse.*

About thirty minutes later, Bobby walked out of Mrs. Lewis's office. He purposely turned the other way, avoiding eye contact with me.

- 23 -

"Caleb, please come back in here," Mrs. Lewis called from her office.

I reluctantly stood, walked into her office, and slumped down in the chair. I knew this was the moment when I would hear my punishment.

"Caleb, typically I would suspend you for three days for starting a fight at our school," she said.

Her words stung deep. *Three days. How embarrassing! How will I ever fix this?*

She added, "However, I talked to Bobby, and he insisted that I not suspend you."

I sat in complete shock. *I would have wanted him suspended forever if he had taken a cheap shot at me in front of the entire class. What is the Blade-*

The Golden Puck

breaker trying to get now? Does he want me off the hockey team instead? Or suspended for a portion of the season?

"This is truly a rare case; you are such a fine young man, Caleb. But something has to be done," she said.

I nodded in agreement. I knew I needed some sort of correction so I could start to move on from my terrible decision.

"So what kind of discipline are you considering?" I asked.

"Well, Bobby was the one who actually had the idea," she said.

Great! Now the incredible Bobby is offering advice to our principal on how to discipline kids.

"He came up with the idea, and I agreed to it. As long as you do it, you will not be suspended, and additionally, this incident won't go on your record," she said.

Not suspended and not on my permanent record? Right now, I would do just about anything to make sure that happened.

"Okay, I'm listening," I said.

"Bobby wants to eat lunch with you for the rest of the week—the next four days," she said.

Eat lunch with me?

"And?" I questioned.

"That's it—just the two of you—no one else, none of the Frozen Five or anyone else. Just the two of you will have lunch together for the next four days. Do we have an agreement?" she asked.

I was surprised by Bobby's request. I couldn't believe what I was hearing, but I was so thankful to have a chance to keep this incident off my record. The choice was simple, and I didn't need long to answer Mrs. Lewis.

"Okay," I said.

"That means no whispering about him with your friends either. Remember, only the two of you will eat lunch together for the next four days," she said.

"I got it; I promise," I said.

I got up, still numb from the past hour of my emotional roller coaster.

The Golden Puck

Just as I was about to leave her office, I stopped and turned back.

"Mrs. Lewis, thank you for listening to me," I said.

"Caleb, I know your heart," she said.

"Is there anything else I can say or do so you will forgive me?" I asked.

"Honey, I already forgave you before you came in," she said.

"So I don't need to do anything else?" I asked.

"Not for me," she said.

She added, "Caleb, hostility stirs up conflict, but respect and forgiveness cover all wrongs."

"Thank you, Mrs. Lewis," I said.

I added, "Anyway, you don't need to call my parents over today's problem."

- 24 -

I walked into my social studies class late and embarrassed. By now, the entire school knew what had happened during gym class. Mr. Gordon was lecturing about ancient Egyptian waterways when I sat down.

I glanced around and noticed everyone staring at me. I made eye contact with Dalton, who quickly looked away. Behind Dalton was Bobby, listening to Mr. Gordon and still wearing his torn shirt.

After class, Colin ran up to me.

"What is going on, Caleb? I couldn't believe it when you creamed Bobby like that. What was that all about? Did he say something to you?" he asked.

"That was my fault," I said.

The Golden Puck

"The whole school is talking about it," said Colin.

By the end of the day, I was more than ready for school to end. I was relieved when the final bell rang at three o'clock in the afternoon.

Now it was time for hockey practice.

I had to face Bobby, my team, and my dad. I wasn't looking forward to it at all.

A bunch of us rode the bus to the ice rink after school for practice. I got on quickly and sat against the window. I looked out the window on the way to the rink. I didn't feel like talking to anyone; I was talked out.

This was one practice and conversation with my dad that I wanted to get over with. The anticipation was tearing at me, and I felt terrible about hurting our team and my dad.

Something about being on the ice was magical. Even with all the drama from earlier in the day, I calmed down as soon as my skates hit the ice.

My peaceful skating was interrupted with a sharp whistle. I turned to see Dad standing at the edge of the rink, motioning for me to come toward him.

"Caleb, we will talk after practice. Try being a leader today," Dad said in an assertive tone.

I knew what he meant. I should be a leader at practice because I had failed miserably at school today. I could tell that Dad was very upset. I didn't blame him and felt bad that I had put him in a bad spot. I was his son, our team leader, and I had acted totally out of character.

I tried to block out the day's happenings and practice hard, which for the most part I did. Our team was really into practice, and this one seemed like our best practice of the year. I think part of their performance was due to the fact that everyone knew my dad was already in a bad mood because of my stunt at school. The other reason was that the next day was November 15 and practically a holiday for those of us who live in the thumb of Michigan. November 15 is the opening day of firearm deer hunting and a rich tradition in Bad Axe.

The Golden Puck

November 15 also meant no school and no hockey practice! Most of our team members planned on spending the day in the woods hunting with their dads.

I love deer hunting and was thankful that opening day came at the perfect time. I needed a break from school and hockey.

Also, I would have to have lunch with Bobby one less day. Mrs. Lewis must have forgotten about that "holiday" today when we were talking. Instead of four lunches with Bobby, it meant only three.

I left practice sore and tired. My head hurt, and I didn't feel great. After the day that I had endured, I felt exactly how I should.

I waited for Dad in the car, worried about how angry he would be. He did a good job at practice being a coach and not Dad. I didn't push my luck and worked extremely hard during practice to make it go as smoothly as possible.

After waiting several long minutes, I saw Dad walking toward the car. He got in and started the car without saying a word.

Wow...he's madder than I thought.

I went to say something to him, and he held up his hand, stopping me.

"Caleb, I don't think it's a good time. I don't want to say something I will later regret," he said.

The rest of the car ride home, we both sat in silence. I stared out the window, wondering when my dad was going to talk to me. A light rain was making the landscape blurry.

When we got home, I showered and went right to my room. Not wanting to cry again, I avoided my mom. I didn't know if I could hold myself together if she was upset.

Finally around eight o'clock in the evening, I heard a low knock on my door.

I knew it was my mom.

She walked in and sat on my bed.

"Caleb, I know you had a rough day today. Dad said he will talk to you about it tomorrow in the hunting blind—when you guys have some quiet time with each other," she said.

I nodded. Mom was one of the most loving,

sincere people I had ever known, and I knew I had disappointed her.

She stood and left my room.

I set my alarm. The thought of tomorrow morning being opening day brought momentary excitement. However, sitting in a hunting blind with my upset dad was something I wasn't looking forward to.

- 25 -

The smell of bacon and the crackling sound of grease on the stove woke me. I looked around the darkness of my room and noticed I had forgotten to close my blinds last night. It was still dark outside, so it didn't matter.

I rolled over and glanced at my LED alarm clock. The numbers glowed a bright red. Strangely, this morning the numbers were blurred.

The batteries must be getting bad or something. I grabbed the clock, and drawing it closer to my eyes, I could finally make out the time: 4:15 a.m.

I threw on a pair of sweatpants and a faded Michigan Wolverines hoodie I had lying on my dresser.

The Golden Puck

"Morning, Son," Dad said as I walked toward the table.

I stumbled into the chair, still half asleep.

He loaded my plate with bacon and chocolate chip pancakes, our typical opening day breakfast. Sipping his coffee, he sat down with me.

He went over the weather and the whitetail bucks he hoped we would see and get a shot at. I listened happily. As of yet, he had made no mention of the school incident yesterday.

The anxiety was still weighing heavily on my chest. I knew it was only a matter of time before we would rehash my horrible day.

The crisp November Michigan morning was picture-perfect. Our boots crunched against the frost as we walked to our hunting shack on the edge of a harvested cornfield. We had a really good hunting spot. Last year I had shot a seven-point buck on opening day. Bagging that buck was one of my greatest memories with my dad. He was so proud of me that morning. I had no doubt he felt much different about me this opening morning.

When we reached the hunting blind, it was still dark. I crawled up the ladder to the shack by feeling each step. My eyes hadn't adjusted to the darkness, and the moon was hidden behind clouds.

I sat in the dark, waiting for my dad to talk, but he didn't. I knew he didn't want to scare away any deer, but I could also tell he was searching for the right words to say.

Just at daybreak, I felt Dad reach over and tap my left leg. I turned toward him. His eyes were wide, and he was motioning to my right. I turned but couldn't see any deer.

"Caleb! Right there, eight-point buck," Dad whispered.

I squinted. We had reached that weird time when it wasn't exactly light out, but the sun was breaking on the horizon.

"I don't see it," I whispered back.

"Right there—like 40 yards away under the first apple tree. How can you not see him?" Dad asked.

I couldn't see any deer! I lifted my rifle and used my scope to scan the entire edge of the field.

The Golden Puck

"I still don't see anything," I said.

"He's gone now, but he was right there, Caleb. You've got to be ready! A buck isn't just going to stand there all day!" Dad said in a disgusted voice. I knew Dad's sarcasm was only frustration; he really wanted me to bag another buck.

I was ready. At least I thought I was. We sat there waiting for another chance. The sun poked through the clouds, and we heard random gunshots all around us.

My dad seemed irritated that I had not seen the buck. We sat for the next couple hours in silence. Every once in a while, Dad would fidget and turn in my direction.

I knew he wanted to talk about yesterday. So every time he looked toward me, I would pick up my binoculars like I had seen something.

That ruse bought me some time. Around 10:30 a.m. we got up and headed back to the truck. We had planned on meeting some friends at a local restaurant to swap hunting stories and eat lunch.

Dad started the engine and slowly backed out

of the hayfield where we had parked. After about a mile, he turned to me.

"Okay, let's stop playing this game. Tell me what happened yesterday," he said.

Yesterday? Did he really think what happened yesterday was all about one day? No, it was a build-up of disappointments and letdowns.

How could I tell him everything I wanted to share? It wasn't just about yesterday; it was about everything! My entire year was off to a horrible start—all because of Bobby…because my dad let him be on our hockey team.

I knew something my dad hadn't yet realized. I had finally come to the conclusion that I blamed all this mess on the Bladebreaker…and my dad too!

- 26 -

At one time I had just wanted to avoid everything all together, hoping maybe it was all a bad dream that would simply go away.

But now riding with my dad in his truck, it was time to let it all out—everything.

For a moment, telling Dad everything felt great. A couple times I had to stop because I was on the verge of crying. I even brought up how Bobby walked into the lunchroom with Kelly.

To my surprise, Dad listened without interrupting or making any faces. I was reading his body language as I told him how Bobby had ruined my life at school, practice, and everywhere else he went.

Then I looked him square in his eyes and told him he was also part of the problem. "The Bladebreaker would never be at Bad Axe if you hadn't let him try out for our hockey team."

"Caleb, I am so sorry that you feel this way," said Dad. I could tell I had gotten his attention and opened his eyes to everything that had changed for me in such a short period of time. For one of the first times in my life, the king of pep talks, random motivational quotes, and stories was speechless.

We pulled into the restaurant, and as I reached for the handle, Dad stopped me.

"Caleb, I can see this has been much tougher on you than I thought. I admit, I was so consumed with getting our team ready to win that I didn't even think about how it affected you personally. You're right; that's on me," he said.

"But, Caleb, when it comes to Bobby, don't assume everything is great on his end. Moving to a new school is hard, Son. Try to cut him some slack."

Cut him some slack? Did he not listen to every-

thing I just told him? The Bladebreaker was arrogant and rude, and now he was taking over everything I loved.

I figured I was in no position to bargain or argue with my dad. I nodded, got out of the truck, and walked into the small diner. I felt better knowing that I had just vomited out all of my feelings to my dad. What I shared wasn't pretty, but our conversation was something that needed to happen.

At school the next day, Dalton ran up to me first thing in the morning.

"What happened? Did your dad ground you for life?" Dalton asked.

"Nothing. We talked," I said.

"Huh? Your dad just talked to you about it? Like you didn't get in any trouble?" Nathan questioned.

I turned toward Nathan and realized I was surrounded by the Frozen Five. They all wanted to know how I had gotten out of this one.

My dad had coached them for the past five years, so they all knew how intense he was. To be honest, I was surprised that the conversation never came up again when we were hunting last night or at home.

For some reason, Dad left it alone—no lecture, no punishment. He just didn't bring it up again.

"I don't know, but all I know is, I am ready to move on. I'm ready to quit talking about it," I said, walking away, annoyed by their constant questions.

"Maybe he will talk to both of you guys tonight at practice," said Lucas.

I stopped. *I never thought of that! The last thing I want to do is sit and talk with Dad and Bobby. That scenario had never entered my mind.*

Lucas brought up a good point. Maybe Dad is waiting to talk to both of us and make me apologize to Bobby in front of the whole team.

I suddenly realized that my problem wasn't going to go away on its own. I worried about hockey practice the rest of the day during school.

Pizza Day was a big day for us; we loved it. Most of the time, we each bought seconds at lunch to get an extra pizza. Not today though. I walked in, grabbed my lunch, and sat down next to Bobby. I didn't say a word, and neither did he. I poked at my pizza without ever taking a bite. My mind raced as I finally walked to the trash can, threw away my entire lunch, and left.

One down, two more days to go until I can eat with the Frozen Five again.

The rest of the school day I thought about what I would say to Bobby at practice. I wanted to be ready when Dad called both of us out.

If my dad wants to bring it all up and make me apologize to Bobby, I will at least let Bobby know all the pain he's caused me since moving to Bad Axe and becoming a Barn Burner.

- 27 -

I hesitantly skated onto the ice without making eye contact with my dad or any of the other coaches. I purposely waited longer in the locker room so most of the team would already be on the ice for practice.

I skated around for a couple minutes before Dad blew the whistle.

"Offensive players, blue line puck handling; defensive players, other end with Coach Smith," Dad yelled.

Maybe he's going to wait until the end of practice to bring it up.

I skated toward the blue line and waited.

Nathan looked at me with a strange expression.

The Golden Puck

Then before I knew it, other players were staring at me as I waited for Dad to bring some pucks.

After a couple of awkward minutes, Dad skated over.

"Caleb, what are you waiting for?" he asked in an irritated voice.

Annoyed, I looked at him.

"Just for you to bring the pucks," I said. I looked around and noticed strange looks on the faces of all the other players.

Dad looked down at the ice in front of me.

"Caleb, the pucks are right in front of you," he said in a concerned tone.

I looked down and scoured the ice; I didn't see any pucks.

"Son, come over here for a second," Dad said, motioning me toward the side of the ice.

I skated over, feeling confused.

"Caleb, can you *not* see the pucks?" he asked.

I looked up at him and shook my head.

A look I had never seen before spread across my dad's face.

"Okay, Son, let's get back to practice," he said. The rest of hockey practice felt normal, and I wasn't sure why Dad was so sensitive about my not seeing a couple of hockey pucks.

When practice ended, I stayed on the ice, getting extra reps working on puck handling. I had one of my best practices of the year. I was really feeling the puck well with my stick. *I want to be prepared for the next tournament.*

We were scheduled to play the Turkey Classic in Grand Rapids the weekend before Thanksgiving.

I also didn't want to give Dad an opportunity to corner Bobby and me. The last thing I wanted to do was talk to the Bladebreaker. I hoped time would pass and the incident would not come up again.

Dad was quiet on the way home. We walked into the house, and I headed to the shower. I could hear Dad talking to Mom about something that sounded important. After my shower, Dad called me to join them at the kitchen table.

"Son, I want you to know that your mom and I love you a lot. We are proud of you," he said.

"Thanks, Dad," I responded cautiously, waiting for the punchline. *Is Dad setting me up for my punishment after talking to Mom?*

"But lately your mom and I have been noticing some—" he started.

"Dad," I interrupted, "I know I haven't been myself. The whole Bobby thing—I am just going through a rough patch. I'm fine," I said.

"Caleb, it doesn't have anything to do with hockey or that new boy," Mom said softly.

"Caleb, your mom just got off the phone with the University of Michigan Hospital. You have an appointment tomorrow," he said.

U of M Hospital? Appointment tomorrow? What is going on? Why can't I just go uptown to Bad Axe and visit my doctor?

"Like with a shrink or something? I told you, I'm fine with everything," I said. *The last thing I need is some psychologist asking me about my feelings.*

"No, Caleb, nothing like that," Dad said. Only this time his eyes told me a different story.

This is something serious. I knew something major was happening.

"It's about your eyes," Dad said.

The strange thing was, I felt a piercing pain in my chest when he said it.

Going to U of M Hospital is serious. I know something is not quite right with my vision.

The next day we would have to get up early to drive to Ann Arbor and see a doctor at the University of Michigan Hospital.

Hockey quickly became an afterthought that night. I knew Dad wasn't going to bring up my school incident with Bobby.

I had a bigger problem to worry about. The past few months I had been full of anger and frustration with the Bladebreaker. I had wasted so much time and energy on worrying about Bobby. The only positive part about going to the hospital was having to sit with Bobby in the lunchroom one less day this week. I would only have one day left.

Little did I know, my battle was just beginning…

- 28 -

Getting up so early the next morning was rough. We rolled out of the driveway at 5:15 a.m., and I was already exhausted. I slept for most of the two-and-a-half-hour trip to Ann Arbor.

I didn't ask any questions even though I had a million running through my mind. I was worried, and so were my parents; I could hear the concern in their voices.

Sitting in a cold, bright-white waiting room didn't help with the anxiety of the situation. My stomach knotted and twisted while waiting to meet with a doctor I didn't know.

The fact that we were able to get in so quickly was also a sign that whatever was happening with my eyes was not good. Usually, scheduling an appointment to get into the U of M Hospital meant a long wait, but somehow I got in the next morning after my mom had called.

We were called back to a smaller room. I answered basic questions as the nurse took my blood pressure and temperature.

A couple minutes later, the doctor walked in. Tall and lean, he looked like a former U of M football player. He had broad shoulders and a calm smile.

Introducing himself as Dr. Howard, he asked me some questions and then turned to my parents.

I sat sick with worry, waiting to hear what was going on.

He left the examination room several times. At one point, a nurse took some blood samples. Throughout my appointment time, several other medical personnel stopped in the room to speak with my parents. I went through a battery of eye exams and a number of tests.

Dr. Howard returned at the end of the day,

rolled over in a chair, and sat directly in front of me. He was close, which I appreciated because I was having trouble seeing him clearly.

He talked very slow and deliberate as he looked directly at me. I could see tears welling up in Mom's eyes. Dad seemed upset and angry.

I just sat quietly and listened. Dr. Howard used some pretty big words, and I didn't know what it all meant. I did know it wasn't good. Even though most of the words were sophisticated and advanced, I caught several key words. As Dr. Howard talked, the world around me froze. I could see his lips moving and hear his voice, but my mind went into complete shock as I heard words like *optic neuropathy, inherited, disease, and legally blind.*

"In most cases," Dr. Howard said, "this condition starts around the age of fifteen and is the leading cause for vision loss. There is no treatment, and at the onset of the problem, there is no way to reverse the condition. While I cannot give you an exact range, possibly Caleb will have 10 percent to

15 percent of his vision, which is considered legally blind."

His diagnosis cut through me.

My mind screamed. *I'm not going to be able to see? How can that be? How will I live? What about my hopes and dreams?*

Dr. Howard added, "Within a matter of months, Caleb's vision will be gone."

The vibrant, colorful world I see will soon fade away. I'm losing my vision; I'm going to be blind…

-29-

Mom sat with me in the backseat and held me the whole way home as I slept and cried.

How could I lose my sight? Everything I love involves seeing...

Hockey? How would I ever play hockey again?

I was so distraught that Mom just held me, and I felt her tears on my cheek.

I was filled with shock and anger.

When we got home, I went directly to my room and to my bed. I was mentally worn out. I looked around the room, taking a mental inventory of everything because the day was coming when I wouldn't be able to see it anymore.

My head ached from crying and the long day at

the hospital. My cell phone kept buzzing with messages. For the first time in my life, I shut it off.

That night I was completely exhausted and fell into a deep sleep. When I woke up the next morning, my pillow was covered in drool. I suddenly knew I had slept in. I grabbed my alarm clock and saw it was now 11:40. I jumped up and ran toward the kitchen.

"Mom, I'm late for school," I shouted. I ran around frantically grabbing my homework and looking for my book bag.

"It's okay. I am letting you stay home today," she said in her quiet voice.

In all the panic of the moment, I had forgotten about yesterday's devastating news.

I thought it was another normal day, but it wasn't. It was Thursday, two days before the Thanksgiving Hockey Tournament. Typically, my heart would have been racing with excitement to play hockey.

"I'm going back to bed," I quickly said, realizing my new reality.

"Okay, Son," my mom said softly. I really appreciated the fact that my parents were giving me some time to try to cope with the news.

I turned on my phone. I had over fifty messages. I saw the Frozen Five were blowing it up. Then I realized that the rest of the world knew my devastating news, and I wasn't in the mood to hear people tell me how sorry they were for me.

I stared at the ceiling as questions bombarded my mind.

Why me? I have so much of my life yet to live.

I cried as I thought of all that I loved to see on the ice—a perfect stick pass and the puck slamming past the goalie in the back of the net. Other images raced through my mind.

I thought about the many little incidents—the times when I ran into things or didn't see things. I just never thought anything of it.

I fell asleep again. I woke up later in the afternoon when I heard a knock on my door. Dad walked in.

"Time to get up, Son. We have hockey practice in twenty minutes," he said.

"Hockey practice?" I said.

"Yeah, big tournament this weekend," he said.

Why is Dad acting like everything is fine and normal?

"Dad, didn't you hear the doctor? I'm done with hockey, done with seeing. I am going to be blind!"

I could tell the words stung my dad. I'm sure it was difficult for him to hear me sobbing.

Dad drew a deep breath. I could tell he was trying his hardest to hold it all together.

"Not yet, you're not! You can still play this season," he said in a caring tone.

"What's the point, Dad? Huh? Really, what's the point? My hockey career is over. Everything I love is going to change," I said, sobbing.

"Okay, Son," Dad said, giving me a hug as he left my bedroom.

I was going to stay there for a while. I had no plans to ever play hockey again.

-30-

"Are you sure you don't even want to go watch? Those are your best friends and teammates," Mom said the next morning.

"I just can't, Mom. I'm not ready," I said.

I sat at the table that Friday morning, wondering how so much could change in a matter of two days. Instead of getting ready to play hockey, I sat in my pajamas, staying home from school for another day. I knew the entire team would be leaving for Grand Rapids after school for the hockey tournament.

"I think maybe it would be good if you came—even if all you do is watch," Dad finally said.

"Watch? Sit there and watch all my team play

when I was supposed to be out there with them?" I asked.

"You can still play, Caleb! The doctor even said he doesn't know how fast everything will happen," said Dad.

"But it's going to happen. It's already happening, Dad," I snarled. I knew my parents were showing me grace by not responding to my surly attitude.

"It's your choice, but I know the guys would love to see you," he said.

"I am not going; I am never going to play hockey again!" I yelled, racing back to my room.

I heard Dad get up from the table and walk by my room.

"I love you, Son," was all he said as I saw his shadow underneath my door. *What could he say? There's nothing anyone can say.*

That weekend was one of the longest weekends of my life. I mostly stayed in my room, only coming out to eat and use the bathroom. Every once in a while, Mom would come in and check on me. She was sweet and protective.

The Golden Puck

"The boys won the first game 5-2 and the second 4-3. Dad wanted to let you know they miss you," she said.

"Thanks for the update," I said. I had cried so much the past couple days I didn't think I had any tears left.

On Saturday afternoon, I started feeling stiff and uncomfortable from lying down so much. I got up and turned on my video game system and sat on the end of my bed.

I waited a couple minutes, staring blankly at the television waiting for the game to start, but nothing was happening. I got up and walked over to the machine to make sure everything was plugged in when I noticed the start screen was now up.

I went back and sat down, ready to play.

I stared at the same apparently blank screen.

It wasn't blank; in fact, the game was on like it should have been.

I slammed my controller on the bed in anger. My eyes had gotten even worse. *Now I can't even see my video games.*

Hearing the noise, Mom walked in to check on me.

"Is everything okay?" she asked.

"No, nothing is okay," I yelled, somehow finding more tears.

Through my crying, I added, "I can't even see my video games anymore."

Mom walked over and wrapped her arm around me.

"Just move closer. Get a chair and move closer," she whispered. I walked over to grab a chair from my desk, positioning it in front of my television. I was much closer, so I could make out the video game enough to play it.

For now, Mom had found a simple solution that allowed me a little joy and took my mind off the hockey tournament my team was playing in.

- 31 -

Sunday night Dad returned home and handed me a huge gold trophy from the Turkey Classic.

Even as upset as I was, holding that trophy felt good.

"The team dedicated this weekend's tournament to you, Caleb. They wanted you to know that they love and miss you," said Dad.

He added, "I really missed you out there this weekend, Son."

I missed it too—not just the hockey, but the hotels, the joking, and being with my friends. Being part of a team is wonderful, especially when the team is made up of your best friends in the whole world.

I sat on the couch, holding the big heavy trophy.

"Don't stay up too late; you have school tomorrow," Dad said as he walked into the kitchen.

"School?"

"I don't know if I am ready," I quickly shot back.

"Ready or not, you need to be in school," Dad responded.

I knew I would have to face all my friends and classmates sooner or later, but I was planning on it being much later.

"Dad, we only have three days of school this week, then we have three days off for Thanksgiving. Please let me stay home a couple more days," I pleaded.

"I think going to school is a good idea, honey," Mom said from across the room.

"Caleb, none of us like what is going on. But it is something we have to start dealing with," said Dad.

"I know, Dad. I have been trying to deal with it ever since the doctor said it, but Dad, please. Just a couple more days… I promise I will go back after the break," I said.

The Golden Puck

Dad paused and thought about my request.

"Okay, this week, but you will be in your seat next week after Thanksgiving break—no exceptions," he said.

"Promise," I said.

I had bought myself another week of avoiding people. My mind was already reeling with ways to extend my time at home or to avoid going back to school altogether.

"And no, you're not doing school online or anything. You will be back in school next week!" Dad said.

Thanksgiving was a special time in our house. Our relatives come over and fill the house with noise and laughter. I looked forward to it every year. This year I only wanted to get through it. I knew my entire family loved and cared for me, but I didn't want the day to be awkward. One of my favorite traditions was our entire family of thirty filling our living room to cheer for the Detroit Lions. I enjoyed the cheers and boos during the football game; the room was always loud and fun.

But this year was going to be different.

I didn't want my family to treat me any differently than they had in the past. I knew everyone was going to want to talk to me about what was going on. But I didn't want to talk to them; I simply wanted them to treat me like they always did. The last thing I wanted was pity or sadness.

Thanksgiving morning I woke up to the smell of stuffing and turkey. The smell dispersed throughout the house and somehow made its way into my bedroom. I rolled over with a smile as the delicious aroma became my alarm clock.

I walked into the kitchen and greeted Mom. I looked at the microwave and noticed it was already 10:30 a.m.

"Mom, you let me sleep in?" I questioned.

"Yes, Honey. You seemed tired," she said, opening the oven and pulling out some freshly baked rolls.

"What time will everyone be here?" I asked.

"Around eleven o'clock the relatives will start showing up. We plan to start eating around noon," she said.

The Golden Puck

I scrambled back toward my bedroom. I barely had time to shower and get ready. I ran to my closet, frantically searching for my Detroit Lions jersey—the same one I had worn the past two seasons.

When I got to the closet, I struggled to make out all the clothes. My eyes were having trouble focusing, and I was getting frustrated.

"It's right here," Dad said. I turned back toward him as he reached to grab the Honolulu blue jersey that had been hanging right in front of me.

I didn't see it. I know my eyes are getting worse. I'm losing my sight, and no one can do anything about it.

- 32 -

I stayed in my room, trying to hide as the family started to arrive for Thanksgiving. I could hear the doorbell ringing and then loud conversations.

Our house began to fill up with people and excitement.

"You can't hide all day, all of your life," I told myself, finally mustering up the courage to leave and greet family.

I slowly walked out of my room and was greeted with hugs and hellos. Apprehensively, I waited for someone to mention something about what was happening.

To my surprise, no one acted weird or brought up the fact that I was going to be blind. I was greet-

The Golden Puck

ed with the typical hugs and high fives. The only time I thought about my diagnosis was when my grandma hugged me. She held me a little tighter and longer than usual. It was her way of showing that she knew how hard everything was. We sat down to eat, and after Dad prayed, the house erupted with conversations.

For a short time, I forgot about all the bad stuff and just felt good. About forty of our relatives came, so our house was full. A couple of cousins my age had come, and we always got along well even though I didn't see them as much as I wanted to. They lived on the west side of the state in Grand Rapids, about three and a half hours from our house in Bad Axe.

After dinner, we enjoyed my favorite part of the day—dessert.

There is nothing in this world I love more than my grandma's homemade pecan pie. I cut a huge slice, and before digging in, I took a deep whiff, inhaling the nostalgic Thanksgiving smell.

That pie smelled delightful!

As my eyes were failing me, I realized my other senses were seemingly getting sharper. I could hear better, and my sense of smell had increased.

That pie tasted so good.

I heard my Uncle Kevin screaming in the living room and headed that way. It was almost time for the Lions football game. Seating was always on a first-come basis, so my being late meant I had a seat near the back of the room.

I sat down, still enjoying my pecan pie.

"That guy is macho!" my cousin Deacon said, leaning toward me. I lifted my head to look at the giant big-screen television affixed to our living room wall.

"Do you like him?" he asked.

"Like who?" I asked, squinting at the television.

Deacon paused and quickly changed the subject. At first I didn't understand until I looked toward the television once again. I couldn't tell who on the screen was who. I could see colors and what looked like blurry players moving on the screen.

The Golden Puck

I couldn't watch the game from my seat. A sudden feeling of panic and fright came over me, reminding me quickly of the big problem I had.

My life had changed so much already and was continuing to change at a rapid pace. The worst part was, there was nothing any doctor or anyone could do to stop the progression.

"Caleb, come sit by me," I heard my Papa say. I loved my grandfather, whom I always call Papa.

I looked up and noticed the seat next to him on the couch in the front of the room was suddenly vacant. My dad had gotten up and was standing near me.

I moved to the couch and sat next to Papa. The closer seat definitely helped, and I could see the game much better. I could see well enough to know who had the ball and catch glimpses of the game.

Papa leaned over and squeezed my leg. "I wanted to sit by you anyway," he said with a smile.

I smiled, but I was obviously shaken. The rest of the day was filled with screams and cheering as our Detroit Lions won in overtime, beating the

Buffalo Bills 37-34. It was a great game and made Thanksgiving much more special.

When the game was over, the families started leaving. After our goodbyes, I noticed my grandparents were still there. Typically, they were one of the first ones to leave, but not this time.

The day had been long, and I headed to my bedroom to lie down. I wanted to relax and listen to some music. Just as I was putting on my headphones, I heard a knock on my door.

Papa walked in and sat on the edge of my bed.

"Caleb, I wanted to tell you that I know what you're going through cannot be easy," he said.

"Yeah, it has been tough," I said.

I loved my Papa, and a part of me was relieved that he stayed around to talk to me privately.

"Close your eyes, Caleb," he said.

"Why? Papa, I don't see that well," I said with a slight chuckle.

"Just do it for Gramps," he said with his loving smirk.

"Okay," I said, closing my eyes.

The Golden Puck

"Hold out your hand," he said.

I held out my hand and felt the shaft of my hockey stick.

"What do you see?" he quietly asked.

I sat in total darkness, not knowing or understanding what he meant. Then I started to squeeze and really feel the stick in my hand.

Memories and images of playing hockey filled my mind. Suddenly, I was no longer sitting on my bed. I was on the ice.

I could feel the cold and the glisten of the ice.

Holding that stick felt so good! It was the first time I had touched one since I found out about my diminishing eyesight.

"Caleb, you can still see. It's just going to look different," he said as he stood and left my room.

- 33 -

The house was quiet after a busy Thanksgiving Day. I got up and walked out into our living room. I turned toward my dad who was reading the newspaper on the couch.

"I think I want to play next weekend," I said firmly.

A big, bright smile filled my dad's face.

I headed back to my room and crashed on my bed. The thought of lacing up my skates and ripping across the ice excited me once again.

Can I see well enough to skate? Can I even help the team win? I wondered.

I fell asleep dreaming of playing hockey. I mostly stayed in my room the rest of the week-

The Golden Puck

end. I tried imagining what school would be like now. The last thing I wanted was for people to feel sorry for me or talk to me about what was happening. Sunday we hung out in the living room and watched a movie.

The next morning I mustered all the strength I had and headed into school. There I was greeted by the Frozen Five waiting for me by my locker.

"Are you back?" Dalton questioned.

"I'm going to try to play in this weekend's tournament," I said, trying not to smile.

The next thing I knew, the guys were hugging and cheering for me.

"We got this for sure now," said Colin.

"Guys, I am not what I used to be," I said, brushing off their enthusiasm.

"You're Caleb Geiger, our captain, and one of the best hockey players in the world," said Nathan.

I couldn't help but smile.

"The details don't matter; you will be back on the ice with us this weekend. We are winning the Golden Puck," said Lucas.

This was the first time since my diagnosis that I was excited. The Frozen Five would walk down the halls of school with our heads held high.

The guys left, and I grabbed my books from my locker and headed toward my first-hour math class. I had become familiar with using my hands to feel my way around the halls, which helped make up for my vision loss.

As I turned the corner to head toward my math class, I ran full steam into someone, and the collision knocked all my books out of my hands. I was embarrassed and quickly scrambled to pick up the books, hoping it wouldn't make a big scene.

I felt around for the books and grabbed the ones within reach.

"Here you go, Caleb," said a familiar voice.

It was the Bladebreaker.

My excitement shifted toward anger and frustration when I heard Bobby's voice. I reached over and pulled the books out of the Bladebreaker's hand.

"Caleb, I am sorry—" He wanted to say more, but I cut him off.

The Golden Puck

"Don't be sorry. The last thing I want is your sympathy," I snapped.

"I was going to say I was sorry for running into you," said Bobby.

I squeezed the books so I wouldn't drop them and headed to class.

I did not want or need people to act differently and feel bad for me. The last thing I wanted was added attention from people.

The rest of the day I tried to focus on getting caught up on all my classes from the time that I had missed. When the final school bell rang at three o'clock, I knew I would have a whole new set of challenges.

The time had come for me to get back on the ice.

Getting back on the ice would provide some comfort, but I was worried about hockey for the first time in my life. Hockey had always been something I looked forward to playing; it was my passion.

For the past couple weeks, hockey had not been a part of my life.

Lane Walker

Now, at least for one week, I was a hockey player again. At least that was my thought as I headed to practice. My vision was getting worse, but at least I had one more chance to put on my *Barn Burner* uniform.

One more chance to be a hockey player.

-34-

I drew a deep breath as I skated onto the ice. The cold air filled my lungs, and I felt like I was home.

I loved being on the ice. The past couple weeks of not having that experience made the feeling even more powerful.

I skated a couple laps and was surprised how quickly my body adjusted to being on the ice. I was blazing around the rink.

"Looking good, Caleb," I heard Dad shout.

My vision had deteriorated even more over the past couple weeks. I saw shadows and some color but struggled to make out images that were more than a couple feet from me.

The stick felt great in my hand, and I felt fast on the ice, but the lack of vision was hard to contend with. During a puck handling drill, I completely lost the puck and couldn't find it on the ice. Another time I was racing down the right wing, and Lucas passed me the puck for a wide-open shot on the net, but I never saw the puck coming.

I was a fraction of myself on the ice. Frustrated, I skated toward the locker room and threw my stuff off. I sat on the bench in tears.

I had wanted to win and play in the Golden Puck Tournament so bad. Before I found out about going blind, that tournament was all I thought about.

I now realized this could be the last time I ever played competitive hockey.

If my eyes continue to diminish at this rate, the trip to Calumet might be my last.

I heard the locker room door open and glanced up to see someone walking in my direction. I could tell by his walk that it was my dad—another sign of my deteriorating sight. A month ago I would have been able to see Dad clearly.

The Golden Puck

He sat down next to me and put his arm around me.

"I know this can't be easy, Caleb. This is our new reality. I am heartbroken for you, Son," said Dad.

"That's just it, Dad. I don't want everyone to feel sorry for me. It's still the same Caleb; I just can't see!" I exploded into tears.

"Son, what can I do to help? What do you need?" Dad asked.

"To see! That's what I want, Dad. I want to see again!" I screamed back.

Dad held me as both of us cried on the bench where we had celebrated many times. But not today…this time the bench was a reminder of all that I was losing, including my sight.

"Let's head home, Son. The other coaches will finish practice," Dad said, gathering me in his arms.

We went home, and I went straight to my room. Mom came in a couple hours later. She sat on the end of my bed. I could tell she had been crying.

"Are you okay, Son?" she asked.

"No, Mom, I'm not," I replied truthfully.

"It's okay not to be okay right now," Mom said.

I just lay there staring at the ceiling.

After a couple minutes of silence, Mom stood and walked toward the door. Before leaving, she asked, "Is there anything we can do?"

"I want to stay home this week and not go to the Golden Puck. I am done with hockey forever," I said.

"You can stay home tomorrow, but you will be back in school on Wednesday. You don't ever have to play hockey again if that is what you want," she said, closing my bedroom door behind her.

Her answer was part of the problem. It wasn't that I didn't want to play; I wanted to play more than anything in the world. But I wanted to be able to play *and* see the game around me.

The next day I turned off my phone and slept on and off most of the day. I knew I had to go back to school but was relieved that I wouldn't embarrass myself at hockey practice anymore.

Wednesday morning I walked into school mentally exhausted.

The Golden Puck

I had incorporated some small routines to help me get around at school. I had spent so much time there; I literally knew the layout with my eyes closed.

I could slowly feel the world around me shrinking every day. Sometimes the differences were small, like having to squint to see the whiteboard. More recently I was having trouble recognizing people's faces until they were close to me.

I knew my vision was rapidly deteriorating, and it would be a short time before those shadows turned into darkness.

-35-

"I missed talking to you after practice yesterday," said Lucas as I walked into my second-hour science class.

"Yeah, didn't go well for me on the ice," I said.

"Man, I don't know if I would say that," he said.

"What do you mean? I couldn't even do the puck handling drills; I had trouble seeing the puck," I said.

"Maybe so, but you looked faster than ever. Seriously, you were flying around the ice," he said.

Mr. Coleman started his lesson on photosynthesis, so Lucas turned around quietly.

My mind raced to images of me zooming around the ice. I tried to avoid my friends and ev-

The Golden Puck

eryone else as much as possible. I even ate lunch with my history teacher, Mrs. Simmions. She was a fantastic teacher, loved her students, and always had an open lunch period where kids could go sit and eat with her. I usually never went to her room, but today, I wanted to avoid the lunchroom and the Frozen Five.

"Hello, Caleb, have a seat. We were just talking about inspirational people," said Mrs. Simmions.

I nodded and sat down.

Some girl was talking about Taylor Swift, which was super annoying. Mrs. Simmions was being patient, but I could tell she was looking for some deeper motivation than a pop star.

She went around the room and eventually came to me.

"Caleb, who is someone that inspires you?" she asked.

I thought for a minute and responded, "Probably some hockey player or someone like that," I said halfheartedly.

"Well, you need to dig and find out who and

why. Everyone should have someone who inspires them," she said.

"Can I tell you all about someone who inspires me?" Mrs. Simmions asked the ten kids who were eating lunch with her.

"I read a story once about a man named Erik Weihenmayer. In high school, he was captain of his wrestling team and made it to the championship. As a man, he was even more amazing; he climbed to the summit of Mount Everest and kayaked the Grand Canyon," she said.

All the kids were in awe of his achievements, and so was I. I couldn't imagine climbing the tallest mountain or kayaking the Grand Canyon.

This Erik guy sounds amazing!

The lunch bell rang, and we got up to head for our fourth-period class. I stood and was heading for the door when Mrs. Simmions called me back into her room.

"Thanks for having lunch with us today, Caleb. I know you haven't had the easiest month," she said.

The Golden Puck

"No, I haven't. I enjoyed it and needed a little break," I said with a smile.

I quickly added, "Thanks for telling us about that Erik guy; he's pretty amazing. I can see why you think he's inspirational."

Mrs. Simmions paused, making sure the rest of the group had left her classroom, "You know, I didn't even tell the class the best part."

"Oh, yeah? What's that?" I asked.

"Erik is blind," she said.

-36-

A *blind man scaled the highest mountain range in the world and kayaked through the Grand Canyon?*

Erik's incredible story ran through my mind the rest of the day. After school I went home, and Mom was waiting. I could tell she was worried about me. I imagined her all day pacing and hoping that I had a good day.

"How was your day?" she asked as soon as I walked in.

"It was okay," I said.

"Well, okay is better than bad," Mom said. I could see her shoulders settle and a hint of relief flood her body.

The Golden Puck

"Where's Dad?" I asked.

"Honey, he's at practice," she said.

I had totally forgotten about hockey practice that day. Without seeing anyone from the Frozen Five and after hearing about Erik Weihenmayer, practice had been the last thing on my mind.

"Mom, can you take me to practice?" I asked.

Mom looked shocked and confused.

"Caleb, did I hear you right? You want to go to practice? Are you sure?" she asked.

"I am sure, Mom. Please take me," I said.

We loaded up in Mom's SUV and headed to the ice rink. She dropped me off, and I went into the locker room and put on my gear.

I could hear the skates scratching the ice and the loud whistle from the coaches directing the players.

After getting dressed, I skated onto the ice.

Dad skated toward me.

"Caleb, what are you doing?" he asked.

"Dad, I am going to play in the Golden Puck this weekend," I said.

"Okay, sounds like a plan to me," he said.

"Go ahead and get in line with the forwards; they are working on some puck handling drills," he said.

"No, Dad, I don't think I am going to be with the forwards," I said.

Puzzled, Dad looked at me.

"Send me with the defenders. This weekend I'm going to play defense," I said.

A light bulb went off above my dad's head, and he was embarrassed that he hadn't thought of it. While my vision was bad, I could still skate fast and make out basic jersey colors.

I can play defense! I can play in the Golden Puck Tournament!

Being an offensive player my whole life, I had always worked on ways to get around or through a defense. Now my job would be to stop the other team from scoring or advancing the puck into our end.

The rest of the practice, I worked with the defense and enjoyed it.

In the drills, I played well and knew it. Even

though one of my senses was getting worse, my sense of hearing and feeling for the game had improved.

It was almost like I could see plays happening in my mind before they actually happened; I realized I could anticipate the other players' passes and breakaways.

"Glad to have you back," said a voice over my shoulder.

"Appreciate that, Bobby," I said back. The Bladebreaker had been one of the first ones to pat me on the helmet and encourage me during drills.

When the final whistle blew, I had no doubt that I could still play hockey at a high level. Now instead of being a distraction, I was going to help my team at the Golden Puck Tournament.

Dad blew his whistle hard three times, which signaled all of us to skate to center ice. I felt a sense of excitement with the team—a sense of hope.

"We have one more practice tomorrow. Then we leave Friday morning for Calumet. We all know every detail regarding this tournament. I believe if we play together, we have a real shot to win. Barn Burners on three," Dad shouted as we ended practice.

As I sat on the bench, I was amazed at how different the feeling I had now was from the one I had twenty-four hours earlier.

I now had hope—a small glimmer of hope that I could still do the things I loved so much.

Nathan and Colin high-fived me on their way out, and Dalton came to sit next to me.

"So good to have you back. Caleb, you are the best defender I have ever seen," he said.

"Thanks," I said.

"I am proud to be your friend," he said.

"I'm proud to be your friend too," I said with a smile.

Everyone was excited and proud—the spark the team and I needed. Those dark days ahead seemed a little farther away after that practice.

On the car ride home, Dad was talking fast with an air of excitement. I knew he was happy to have me back.

The Golden Puck

"I am proud of you for trying again and never giving up," he said.

"Thanks, I'm proud too. I know Erik would also be proud," I said.

"Erik? Who's Erik?" Dad asked, confused.

"Just a hero of mine," I said with a smile.

- 37 -

The Barn Burners were ready as we loaded our cars on Friday morning. Most of the kids were excited to miss a day of school. I had missed so much school lately, it was starting to seem normal to me. The drive to Calumet from Bad Axe was about eight and a half hours, so we had to leave at eight o'clock in the morning. Our first game was at six o'clock in the evening, so that would give us enough time to check into our hotel and prepare for the game.

Dalton and Colin rode with us. We had fun singing loudly to my dad's radio and playing car bingo.

The farther north we traveled, the more beauti-

The Golden Puck

ful the scenery was. We loved crossing the super-high Mackinac Bridge that connects the lower peninsula to the upper peninsula of Michigan.

As the car rolled over the bridge, Dalton's face was pressed against the window. His breathing was heavy and fogging up the window. The vast expanse of Lake Michigan stretched out all around us. The unusually mild Michigan winter had left the deep blue waters open and wild. Dalton had a huge fear of heights, and I could see him getting more nervous as we ascended the bridge's gentle incline.

Dalton's eyes widened at the sight of the massive steel cables, each one as thick as a tree trunk, supporting the weight of the roadway. The rhythm of the vehicle passing over the bridge's metal structure created a symphony of sound that only added to his fear. After a couple minutes, I could see Dalton was drawn to the bridge.

At the midpoint, it almost seemed like he was enjoying the view and the ride. As we began the descent down the Mighty Mac, the distant shore grew closer and closer. When the car finally hit solid ground, Dalton almost seemed to miss the bridge.

"That was actually kind of cool," he said.

"Yeah, I love the Mackinac Bridge," said Colin.

As I had watched Dalton face his fear, a thought popped into my head. "Sometimes you just have to take the next step, no matter what life throws at you," I said.

"That's pretty good advice," my dad said, glancing in the rearview mirror.

Taking the next step even though life had dealt me a poor hand was exactly what I planned to do this weekend. As I looked in the rearview and the bridge disappeared behind us, I was thankful that I had gotten to view the bridge one more time. *This might be my last time to see it.*

Dad continued to drive toward Calumet; we still had five hours left.

I was so glad that I had chosen to come instead of sitting in my room alone. I wasn't sure if I would be able to help much, but just being part of a team

The Golden Puck

is special. The rest of the ride, I enjoyed being silly with my friends.

It was one of the best rides of my life.

We pulled off of Highway 41 and into the Copper Country Inn in Calumet. This older hotel was full of history.

We quickly unloaded and headed to the Calumet Colosseum and our first game of the tournament. We had a pretty tough draw for the tournament and had to win all three of our games to get into the final and have a chance to win the Golden Puck.

Our first game wouldn't be easy as we had to take on the Edmonton Wolves from Canada. They were a really good team and had finished fourth last year in the tournament.

If we lost Friday night, our dream of bringing home the Golden Puck to Bad Axe would be gone. We had to be focused and play well, or our tournament dreams would be over before they started.

We pulled in the front of the arena, where we were welcomed at a grand entrance. Large wooden doors with intricate carvings greeted us. A vintage marquee displayed the CALUMET COLOSSEUM in bold, upper-case letters, and weathered paint showing countless hours of hockey games.

The roof of the Colosseum is crowned and fitted with a glorious copper dome, an appropriate place to prove yours is the best hockey team.

The copper-colored top of the famous Calumet Colosseum looked amazing, but not nearly as striking as the Golden Puck trophy.

-38-

Walking into the Colosseum was breathtaking. The historic arena didn't disappoint. When we pulled open the large wooden doors, the historic air filled my lungs, and the sounds of skates cutting through ice and the echoes of cheers filled the air.

A familiar scent of hot chocolate and popcorn permeated the arena, wafting through the chilly December air, adding to the excitement.

The sound of the puck clanking loudly against the hockey sticks created a lively atmosphere. I couldn't wait to be a part. I felt a deep sense of belonging to these hallowed hockey grounds.

It was hard not to sense the pride of thousands

of hockey players who had laced up their skates in the Colosseum through the years. I sat in awe, wondering how many players had sat here before me dreaming about hockey—dreaming about winning the Golden Puck.

We could all sense a nervous energy as Dad prepped us for the game. Knowing we were playing the Wolves first and having to win all our games just added to the tension.

A large crowd had gathered in the Colosseum for our game with the Wolves. Our fans traveled well, so the Barn Burner supporters filled up the seats behind our bench. They roared as we took to the ice for warm-ups.

As I skated back and forth across the ice warming up, the usual deep feeling of contentment from gliding across the ice washed over me, and I took a moment to appreciate my decision to come play. I would have had so much regret if I had stayed home in my room all weekend. I was thankful to be there and to be a part of my Barn Burner team.

The game started off with a flurry of shots on

goal by both teams. I sat patiently waiting for my time to go into the game and trying to focus on any of the Wolves players that I would need to stop. While I couldn't read jerseys or recognize faces, I could still see the bright-yellow Wolves jerseys.

Their players were fast and skilled, but so were we. We scored first on a three-on-two break. Colin hit Bobby on the right side with a perfect pass for a goal!

The first period ended, and our team held a 1-0 lead.

During the first intermission, Dad walked over and asked me if I was ready to go in.

"Not yet, but soon. I will let you know," I said.

Dad nodded.

The second period started off with a Wolves' goal in the first thirty seconds. One of their players stole the puck and had a one-on-one opportunity against our goalie. Dalton didn't stand a chance, and the horn blasted, tying the game at 1-1.

The second period ended in a 1-1 tie. The third period would determine the game.

"Caleb, you're in!" Dad said as we headed out for the third period.

"Now?" I asked.

"It's time," he said.

I didn't have time to think and raced onto the ice. The whole moment went by too fast. I took my defensive position and watched Bobby win the face-off.

Our offense was battling when I saw a yellow blur out of the corner of my eye. I turned to skate with him, thinking he had the puck. I raced over and stopped him.

Then I heard screaming from our bench, turned, and saw a yellow shirt streaking directly toward Dalton. I looked down and didn't see the puck.

I had missed the guy with the puck; I didn't see the other player. I took off as fast as could, racing to cut off the Wolves player.

But I was too late. He crossed the puck over twice before putting it in the back of the net.

The horn blew, we were down 2-1, and it was all

The Golden Puck

my fault. I skated over to the bench with my head down.

"I'm sorry, guys. I am so sorry," I said.

"Stop, Caleb. We got this," said Colin.

"Let's go, boys," said Lucas.

"Dad, take me out," I said, skating off the ice.

I sat with my head down, knowing I had just lost our team the chance to win the Golden Puck.

The Barn Burners took the ice, and the clock kept winding down. I leaned over to one of the other players on the bench and asked, "How much time is left?"

"Two minutes," he said.

Great. Now I can live the rest of my life knowing that I am the reason our team lost in the last hockey tournament I ever played in.

It would take a miracle…

- 39 -

Well, come to find out, the miracle we needed would come from number 26, the Bladebreaker. With two minutes to go in the game, Bobby went straight into beast mode.

The referee dropped the puck, and Bobby took the face-off and raced toward the Wolves' net. When two Wolves players rushed to cut him off, Bobby stopped and started left before crossing over to his right. The Wolves players ran into each other, and Bobby reached back and took a shot toward the goalie.

The puck flew through the air and glided above the outstretched hand of the goalie.

The horn blasted!

The Golden Puck

The score was now a 2-2 tie with 1:10 left in the game. The Wolves called a time-out. Our guys raced over cheering.

"Great job, Bobby. Boys, we can't tie," Dad said. Suddenly a somber tone went over the enthusiastic team.

"If we tie, we won't make the championship game. We have to win all three games," Dad said.

"Let's win then," said Bobby.

"Okay, we're going to do something crazy. We are going to pull Dalton. But Bobby, you have to win the face-off," said Dad.

Pulling the goalie was an extremely risky move at this point of the game. It would leave us defenseless if they won the face-off. But to our advantage, it would give us an extra player on offense.

"I will win the face-off," Bobby said confidently.

"Let's do it, boys," Dad said.

Bobby faced off with the Wolves' center in the middle of the ice. Just as the referee was dropping the puck, the Edmonton coach began screaming. He noticed we didn't have a goalie.

It was too late.

The puck hit the ice, and Bobby slapped it back toward Colin before streaking toward the goal. Colin corralled the puck and raced down the left wing unguarded, giving us a two on one. After faking a shot to make the defender flinch, Colin fired the puck across the ice to Bobby.

Bobby quickly deked inside and then slid the puck back across the ice to Colin. The poor Edmonton goalie didn't stand a chance. Colin one-timed the puck into the wide-open backside for an easy goal.

The horn sounded, and the announcer blasted, "Number 26 Bobby passed to number 10 Colin for the Barn Burner goal!" *I don't know if I have ever heard a sweeter sound in my life.*

The Barn Burners were 1-0!

I felt better knowing that my mistake had not cost our team the game.

After the game, I walked up to Dad.

"Dad, I tried. You can't play me again. I blew it," I said.

The Golden Puck

"Caleb, it was a tough play, and anyone could have made the same mistake," said Dad.

"I will dress, but don't put me in. I guess I'm not ready," I said.

Dad leaned down and patted me on top of my head.

"Go enjoy the win with your team," he said. With his encouragement, I got up and headed out to join the guys.

Everyone was swarming around Bobby.

"Great game, Bobby," I said.

"Thanks, Caleb," he said softly.

I went into the locker room and changed out of my hockey gear. I took my time, taking off each piece slowly. I knew that I had only a couple more games left as a hockey player, and I wanted to enjoy every second of them.

That night everyone went out to eat, and our time together was a lot of fun. The next morning we played at ten o'clock against the Novi Rams. We won that game easily 5-0, and I dressed but didn't play. Dad and some of the Frozen Five tried to get me to go in, but I just shook my head no. Even though we were winning, I was afraid of making another mistake.

Saturday night at eight o'clock, we played the Green Bay Gators out of Wisconsin. This game went too fast for the Gators, and we won 4-1 pretty easily. I was glad my team was winning. At the same time, I felt somewhat silly sitting there and not doing anything to help our team. Before the game, I had told Dad not to ask because I did not want to play again. He could tell I was serious and respected my decision. None of the other players said anything. I wondered if the coaches had told them to leave me alone about it.

The Barn Burners were 3-0 and were going to play in the championship game on Sunday. The championship game was the highlight of the tournament. The stadium was always packed with people wanting to see some good hockey and eager to find out who would host the Golden Puck trophy.

I went to bed that night grateful that we were

The Golden Puck

one win away and still had a chance to win the championship.

Even though I hadn't helped my team on the ice, I wasn't the reason we lost either.

Now that I was done playing, the pressure was off.

At least that is what I thought. I'm glad I didn't know what was going to happen in the championship game Sunday night.

If I had, I wouldn't have been able to sleep. Little did I know, everything was going to change tomorrow at one o'clock in the afternoon.

- 40 -

Sunday's match was going to feature the two best teams at the Golden Puck Tournament. The tournament had started with twenty-four teams from eight different states on Friday.

Now the tournament was down to only two: the Barn Burners from the little town of Bad Axe, Michigan, and the mighty New York Sharks.

The Sharks were one of the best youth hockey organizations on the East Coast. Their management trained four or five teams per grade level, and we were facing their top team.

Before the game, I could tell all the guys were super nervous.

The locker room was big and had lots of room.

The Golden Puck

I sat my stuff down and began putting on my pads. When I got my shoulder pads on, Nathan called me over.

I left my jersey on the bench and walked toward him. "I want you to know I really miss you on the ice," said Nathan.

"I miss you too. But I will be cheering my head off," I said with a smile.

"I just wanted you to know that," he said.

"Thanks," I said, giving him a side hug and returning to the bench. I reached down, felt my wadded-up jersey, and put it on.

Skating out onto the ice was a moment I will forever cherish. The stands were packed with people. I almost tripped coming out of the tunnel when I saw how many people were at the game. I couldn't really make out who was there; I could only see lots of colors and objects sitting in the stands.

We were doing skating drills when I heard it.

Even as loud as the Colosseum was, I heard the sound of the puck hitting the ice. For the first time ever, I recognized that sound. I looked at center ice and could see the referee practicing dropping the puck as in a face-off. Every time the puck hit the ice, I heard a sharp, distinctive sound.

I could actually see a glow around the puck and then realized I was seeing the official, sacred Golden Puck! The experience was amazing! Playing a game with a solid-gold, 24-carat golden puck was unheard of except at the Calumet Colosseum.

Dad called us together and gave us an amazing pep talk. He talked about how it would take the entire team to win this game, and if we chose to play for each other, we had a shot at greatness. The hair on the back of my neck stood stiff as Dad rallied us together.

The boys took the ice, and I took my spot at the end of the bench. I had made up my mind. Even though I wasn't going to play, I was going to be the best teammate I could be to encourage the guys.

It was clear from the first puck drop that the Sharks had not traveled all the way to Calumet, Michigan, for second place.

They were big, fast, and highly skilled. Our guys

The Golden Puck

needed a couple minutes to get used to the breakneck speed the Sharks played at. Their two defensemen, Caiden and Brock, were the best I had ever seen. They were big and fast, and seemingly, they could read the eyes of opposing skaters and anticipate every move they made. They made it almost impossible for any team to score.

After four minutes of play, we were already down 2-0 and only had one shot on goal. But after the slow start, our guys got comfortable and settled into the game.

I was really into the game and not just because it was for the championship.

The Golden Puck was much louder than other pucks, and its golden color glittered far more than the black puck. Its distinctive sound made it easy for me to track and follow the whole game.

Bobby was able to steal the puck in the Sharks' end of the ice and race in for a goal, making the game 2-1. The second period started off slowly for both teams.

The brash Sharks looked comfortable playing

fast or slow hockey; they were well-coached and disciplined.

Colin, Lucas, and Nathan were having the game of their lives on defense. They were all over the ice. I felt a huge sense of pride, knowing they weren't only playing for each other; they were also playing for me. The whole team was playing well. Bobby was still one of the best players on the ice, and Dalton was doing an amazing job of protecting the net.

The game went back and forth, and the second period ended with the Sharks still leading 2-1. Those two Shark defensemen were unreal; they stopped every scoring chance we had. The puck never even came close to the goalie.

The third period, which was about to start, would determine the winner of the Golden Puck.

As the third period started, I closed my eyes. I could hear the gold puck slamming around the ice and ricocheting off the boards. I knew exactly where the puck was and where it was going.

"Colin, coming your way," I screamed as the

The Golden Puck

puck was heading his way. The other kids on the bench were amazed.

One leaned over. "How did you know that?" he asked.

"I just do," I said. I could hear and see the movements in my mind. This last month had heightened my sense of hearing.

Three minutes into the third period, the Bladebreaker struck again. Bobby put a move on the Shark defender that actually made the opposing player fall to the ice.

Bobby scored to the roar of the crowd and tied the game 2-2.

As the third period dragged on, it was obvious both teams were playing cautiously, trying not to lose the game on a silly mistake.

The puck stayed mostly at center ice, and there weren't many shots on the goal.

Finally, the puck got tied up in the corner, and the referee blew a whistle for a center ice face-off with :30 left in the game.

Dad called a time-out.

The boys skated over exhausted; they had given their all. The Sharks slowly skated to their bench as well. Both teams had given everything they had to win this game.

Dad started to talk about a play when Bobby interrupted him.

"Coach, I have an idea," said Bobby.

"Okay, what's your idea, Bobby?" Dad asked.

"I think you should put Caleb in," he said.

-41-

"Say that again," I said immediately, thinking I had misheard Bobby.

"We are exhausted, and so are they. You are the fastest skater on both teams. You can do it; I know you can, Caleb," he encouraged.

A rush of pride like I had never felt before in life went through my body.

I can do it, and for some reason, I know it too.

"Take the next step," Dalton said, reminding me of what I had told him as we crossed the Mackinac Bridge.

"I can do it," I said, looking at my dad.

A huge smile spread across his face.

"Listen, Bobby, get me the puck. I can hear it;

I will take off to the left wing but be ready. You're getting it back and going to win this game," I said.

The entire team was bursting with enthusiasm!

I knew exactly where Bobby was going to be; I had seen him do it hundreds of times. All I had to do was get the puck past the two Shark star defenders.

My skates hit the ice, and I took my spot on the left side of center ice. Bobby looked at me and nodded slowly.

I closed my eyes.

I didn't need to see the puck; I could hear and feel it.

I heard the clattering sound of the Golden Puck hitting the ice, and I went racing down the left boards. Seconds later I felt a loud thud hit my stick as Bobby sent me the perfect pass.

I pushed and skated harder and faster than I ever had.

I blew past the two fatigued Shark defenders who were totally caught off guard by my fresh legs and speed. They didn't have time to read my next pass. I was too fast, and my eyes were still completely closed.

I had them right where I wanted them.

I knew the goal was close. I heard the faint scratching of blades on the right wing and realized it was Bobby.

All in one motion, I pulled my stick back and rocketed a blind pass toward the right wing. My head never turned, and I never looked in his direction.

I figured the goalie would be so fixated on me that Bobby would have a perfect shot on goal. My blind pass was right on the money as I heard a whooshing sound followed by a whipping sound as the puck slammed into the back of the net.

The horn blew, signaling the goal, then seconds later the buzzer sounded, ending the game.

The Barn Burners won! We were the Golden Puck Champions!

I felt the arms of my entire team grabbing me and tackling me to the ice.

My blind pass was the reason we won the game!

Dad came flying across the ice, slipping and sliding, and fell on top of me.

He was so proud!

I was too!

We lined up for a team picture, and I held the Golden Puck in the middle. I felt the weight of the puck and smiled. I hadn't needed my eyes today—just my ears and my heart!

Everyone was emotional as the announcer called out the names and numbers of the players to receive their medals.

"Number 26, Caleb Geiger," he bellowed.

"Huh?" I leaned toward Dalton.

"We switched your jersey before the game when you went to talk to Nathan," Dalton said.

"The whole game I was wearing number 26?" I asked.

"Yep, it was Bobby's idea," he said.

Bobby the Bladebreaker gave up his jersey so I could wear my number in the championship game?

I skated out, trying to understand everything that had just happened. I felt the official put my

The Golden Puck

medal around my neck. After all the boys were called out, we posed for one last team picture, and then the team started to skate off.

"Let's get a picture with the Frozen Five," Nathan yelled out.

"No," I said.

"Huh? Why not?" asked Lucas.

"How about we get a picture of the *Super Six*?" I asked.

I added, "Bobby, get over here for a picture."

-42-

I was still on cloud nine as we entered the locker room. I sat down, and the place was rowdy with excitement.

I lingered, enjoying every moment.

Bobby walked by toward the exit door.

"Hey, Bladebreaker, you're not such a bad guy after all," I said with a smile.

"There isn't anyone I would rather win with than you," he said, walking out.

The original Frozen Five gathered after everyone had left.

"Don't we need an official vote or something?" Dalton asked.

"No, we don't need a vote; he's in," I said.

The Golden Puck

"Do we all get a vote?" Lucas said.

"Sure, all those in favor of adding Bobby and becoming the Super Six say 'Aye,'" I said.

All five of us exclaimed, "Aye" at once, and it was a 5-0 vote to add Bobby.

"Man, just think!" exclaimed Nathan. "We could all be playing on the same varsity team next year. We could even win State!"

I knew he was just excited and trying to be positive, but I dropped my head.

In all the excitement, we had forgotten about what was happening to me. It didn't need to be said, but at the rate the downward spiral of my sight was happening, I knew that I would probably lose my vision shortly…

"Yeah, maybe," I said, trying to change the somber mood.

The Frozen Five stood up once more and hugged each other. From that point on, we would become the Super Six.

I stayed in the locker room by myself. I looked around and tried to take snapshots of everything I could see. I didn't ever want to forget today. I inhaled deeply, smelling the locker room.

After a couple of minutes, the door opened, and in walked an older man with a washed-out white beard.

"Sorry, I didn't know anyone was still here," he said.

He was a well-dressed man who seemed put together and confident. I had never seen him before.

"Great game, kid," he said, walking over to extend his hand.

We shook hands, and he sat down by me.

"The Golden Puck is one of the best tournaments around," he said.

"Yeah, we have wanted to win this for a long time," I said.

"I just love hockey," said the man.

"Me too," I said.

"Great! Maybe I will see you next year at some other tournaments," he said.

"Yeah, maybe," I said hesitantly.

"You didn't sound too convincing," the man said.

The Golden Puck

"This is probably my last tournament," I said.

"Last tournament? Why? You just said you loved hockey," he said in shock.

"I have this condition that's hard to explain, but I am losing my vision. In a couple months, I will be blind," I explained.

"Oh, I see," the man said. He added, "So why again are you going to be done?"

I sat there looking at him. *Does he not hear me?*

"When you get home, I want you to search the Internet for blind or visually impaired hockey leagues. They are all over the place, and it's high-level hockey. If you love the game, find a way to keep playing," encouraged the man.

With that incentive, he stood to leave and started walking toward the exit door.

"My name is Caleb," I said as he was about to walk out.

The man stopped, turned toward me, and smiled as he said, "My name is Erik. Please tell Mrs. Simmions I said hello."

In a world where sight is often considered to be

the window to understanding, I learned that true vision lies within your heart. I walked out of the Calumet locker room holding the Golden Puck with a smile on my face.

I walked out with far more than a trophy...

About the Author

Lane Walker is an award-winning author, educator and highly sought-after speaker. Walker started his career as a fifth grade teacher before transitioning into educational administration, serving as a highly effective principal for over twelve years. He has coached football, basketball and softball.

Lane paid his way through college working as a news and sports reporter for a newspaper. He grew up in a hunting-and-fishing fanatical house, with his father owning a taxidermy business.

After college, he combined his love for writing and the outdoors. For the past 20 years, he has been an outdoor writer, publishing over 250 articles in newspapers and magazines.

Lane Walker

Walker's Hometown Hunters Collection won a Moonbeam Bronze Medal for Best Book Series Chapter Books. His second series, The Fishing Chronicles, won a Moonbeam Gold Medal for Best Book Series Chapter Books.

Stay tuned! More exciting chapter books by Lane will be released in the future!

Visit:
www.bakkenbooks.com

Local Legends

The Buzzer Beater
The High Cheese
The Storm Blitz
The Last Green
The Game Changer
The Golden Puck

Hometown Hunters Collection

Legend of the Ghost Buck
The Hunt for Scarface
Terror on Deadwood Lake
The Boss on Redemption Road
The Day It Rained Ducks
The Lost Deer Camp

The Fishing Chronicles

Monster of Farallon Islands
The River King
The Ice Queen
The Bass Factory
The Search for Big Lou

For more books, visit: **www.bakkenbooks.com**

Other Bakken Books Stories

Camping books for kids

Mystery books for kids

Hunting books for kids

Fishing books for kids

Made in United States
Cleveland, OH
13 April 2025